U0025487

# The Invisible Man

# 隱形人

Original Author    Herbert George Wells
Adaptor    Louise Benette, David Hwang
Illustrator    Julina Alekcangra

WORDS
800

MP3

# Let's Enjoy Masterpieces!

All the beautiful fairy tales and masterpieces that you have encountered during your childhood remain as warm memories in your adulthood. This time, let's indulge in the world of masterpieces through English. You can enjoy the depth and beauty of original works, which you can't enjoy through Chinese translations.

The stories are easy for you to understand because of your familiarity with them. When you enjoy reading, your ability to understand English will also rapidly improve.

This series of *Let's Enjoy Masterpieces* is a special reading comprehension booster program, devised to improve reading comprehension for beginners whose command of English is not satisfactory, or who are elementary, middle, and high school students. With this program, you can enjoy reading masterpieces in English with fun and efficiency.

This carefully planned program is composed of 5 levels, from the beginner level of 350 words to the intermediate and advanced levels of 1,000 words. With this program's level-by-level system, you are able to read famous texts in English and to savor the true pleasure of the world's language.

The program is well conceived, composed of reader-friendly explanations of English expressions and grammar, quizzes to help the student learn vocabulary and understand the meaning of the texts, and fabulous illustrations that adorn every page. In addition, with our "Guide to Listening," not only is reading comprehension enhanced but also listening comprehension skills are highlighted.

In the audio recording of the book, texts are vividly read by professional American actors. The texts are rewritten, according to the levels of the readers by an expert editorial staff of native speakers, on the basis of standard American English with the ministry of education recommended vocabulary. Therefore, it will be of great help even for all the students that want to learn English.

Please indulge yourself in the fun of reading and listening to English through *Let's Enjoy Masterpieces.*

# 赫伯特・喬治・維爾斯

Herbert George Wells
(1866–1946)

George Wells was born in 1866, in Bromley, Britain. He was the son of an unsuccessful tradesman and a former lady's maid. At the age of thirteen, he left school and became a drapers apprentice, a job his family expected would be proper for him. However, he disliked the job, and his unhappy experiences as a draper were later used as inspiration for his novel *Kipps*. In his early years, Wells used to read everything he could find, while his thoughts were wandering imaginary far-off places and times.

In 1883 he found a job as a teacher's assistant at Midhurst Grammar School. In 1884 he won a scholarship to the School of Science in London, where he was taught by one of the greatest biology teachers of the time, Thomas Henry Huxley, whose influence on his life was extremely powerful. Wells founded and edited the *Science Schools Journal* while at university.

After his graduation in 1888, Wells spent the next few years teaching and writing. In 1891 his major essay on science, *The Rediscovery of the Unique*, was published. In 1895 Wells established himself as a novelist with his science fiction story, *The Time Machine*. The story tells about a dreamer who, obsessed with traveling through time, builds himself a time machine and travels over 800,000 years into the future. The book was so successful that Wells did not need to teach or worry about money from that time on.

Soon after the publication of *The Time Machine*, Wells published other successful novels, *The Island of Dr. Moreau* (1896), *The Invisible Man* (1897), and *The War of the Worlds* (1898). Thus Wells established the modern form of science fiction. He is regarded as the father of modern science fiction and sometimes called the time machine guy. Wells also wrote non-fiction books about politics, technology, and the future, espousing his views on humanity, society, and the direction he saw the world going.

Herbert George Wells died in 1946 at the age of 80, while working on a project that dealt with the dangers of nuclear war. Wells, who dreamed of a more progressive human culture as the forerunner of science fiction novels, still commands the respect and admiration in the world.

## *The Invisible Man*

The story begins with the arrival of a stranger at a British countryside inn on a stormy and cold winter day. In those days, traveling in winter was unusual, but more curiously, the strange man had a bandage wrapped around his face. The whole village was disturbed by the arrival of this strange individual. Then unprecedented incidents began to occur; for example, an unidentified robber broke into Rectory.

Finally, as the landlord and his wife attempted to chase the strange man out of the inn, he unbound the bandage. He revealed himself as an invisible man before a crowd of many people and then immediately disappeared. After much meandering, the invisible man got into the dwelling of Doctor Kemp. Doctor Kemp did not want to tolerate the reckless behavior of the invisible man. Unfortunately, the invisible man was losing his ability to think clearly.

H. G. Wells published this novel in 1897. It represents his classic science fiction novels and depicts a man who invented a medicine capable of making a human invisible. But this invisible man became involved in all kinds of wrongdoings. H. G. Wells portrayed a fantastic scientific discovery. In addition, he deserves recognition for his depiction of the solitary life of an alienated man touched by the depths of despair.

# HOW TO USE THIS BOOK
## 本書使用說明

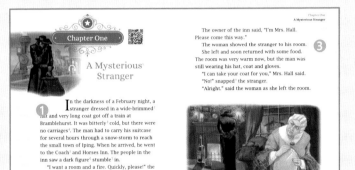

## 1 Original English texts

It is easy to understand the meaning of the text, because the text is rewritten according to the levels of the readers.

## 2 Explanation of the vocabulary

The words and expressions that include vocabulary above the elementary level are clearly defined.

## 3 Response notes

Spaces are included in the book so you can take notes about what you don't understand or what you want to remember.

## 4 One point lesson

In-depth analyses of major grammar points and expressions help you to understand sentences with difficult grammar.

## 🎧 Audio Recording

In the audio recording, native speakers narrate the texts in standard American English. By combining the written words and the audio recording, you can listen to English with great ease.

Audio books have been popular in Britain and America for many decades. They allow the listener to experience the proper word pronunciation and sentence intonation that add important meaning and drama to spoken English. Students will benefit from listening to the recording twenty or more times.

After you are familiar with the text and recording, listen once more with your eyes closed to check your listening comprehension. Finally, after you can listen with your eyes closed and understand every word and every sentence, you are then ready to mimic the native speaker.

Then you should make a recording by reading the text yourself. Then play both recordings to compare your oral skills with those of a native speaker.

# HOW TO IMPROVE READING ABILITY

## 如何增進英文閱讀能力

### ① *Catch key words*

Read the key words in the sentences and practice catching the gist of the meaning of the sentence. You might question how working with a few important words could enhance your reading ability. However, it's quite effective. If you continue to use this method, you will find out that the key words and your knowledge of people and situations enables you to understand the sentence.

### ② *Divide long sentences*

Read in chunks of meaning, dividing sentences into meaningful chunks of information. In the book, chunks are arranged in sentences according to meaning. If you consider the sentences backwards or grammatically, your reading speed will be slow and you will find it difficult to listen to English.

You are ready to move to a more sophisticated level of comprehension when you find that narrowly focusing on chunks is irritating. Instead of considering the chunks, you will make it a habit to read the sentence from the beginning to the end to figure out the meaning of the whole.

## ③ *Make inferences and assumptions*

Making inferences and assumptions is part of your ability. If you don't know, try to guess the meaning of the words. Although you don't know all the words in context, don't go straight to the dictionary. Developing an ability to make inferences in the context is important.

The first way to figure out the meaning of a word is from its context. If you cannot make head or tail out of the meaning of a word, look at what comes before or after it. Ask yourself what can happen in such a situation. Make your best guess as to the word's meaning. Then check the explanations of the word in the book or look up the word in a dictionary.

## ④ *Read a lot and reread the same book many times*

There is no shortcut to mastering English. Only if you do a lot of reading will you make your way to the summit. Read fun and easy books with an average of less than one new word per page. Try to immerse yourself in English as often as you can.

Spend time "swimming" in English. Language learning research has shown that immersing yourself in English will help you improve your English, even though you may not be aware of what you're learning.

# CONTENTS

# Before You Read

## The Invisible Man

I am a cold, impatient[1] man who will kill anyone who tries to stop me. Unfortunately, being invisible is not as easy as I imagined it would be. I need money and clothes to stay warm and well fed[2]. However, every time I try to get these things, I create[3] a lot of trouble for myself. I tried to get other men to help me, but they are afraid of my power. I can't trust anyone.

## Dr. Kemp

I am a simple research[4] scientist who lives in a small seaside town. One day, an old college classmate came to my house quite unexpectedly[5]. You see, this old friend is actually the invisible man! I have to decide whether to help him or to turn him over[6] to the police. He seems to be quite dangerous and capable of[7] killing innocent[8] people to get what he wants.

## Marvel

I was a poor beggar[9] living in the countryside. People ignored[10] me, and I could not find work anywhere. I think that's why the invisible man chose me to help him. However,

I didn't want to help him. He really scared me! After helping him rob[11] a bank, I ran away with the money and his research books. I was so scared he would find me and kill me!

## Mr. Hall and Mrs. Hall

We run[12] a quiet inn in the country town of Iping. We like to have peace but all that was shattered[13] on the night the stranger came. During the weeks he stayed with us, we could hear him losing his temper[14] often and smashing[15] bottles and furniture. He is always covered from head to foot in clothing, even in a warm room. This man is very strange indeed.

1. **impatient** [ɪmˋpeɪʃənt] (a.) 急躁的；不耐煩的
2. **well fed** 飲食充足的
3. **create** [kriˋeɪt] (v.) 引起；產生
4. **research** [ˋriːˌsətʃ] (n.) 學術研究
5. **unexpectedly** [ˌʌnɪkˋspektɪdli] (adv.) 意外地
6. **turn over** 將（某人、某物）交出
7. **capable of** 有……的能力
8. **innocent** [ˋɪnəsənt] (a.) 無辜的
9. **beggar** [ˋbegər] (n.) 乞丐
10. **ignore** [igˋnoɚ] (v.) 忽視
11. **rob** [ˋrɑːb] (v.) 搶劫
12. **run** [ˋrʌn] (v.) 經營；管理
13. **shatter** [ˋʃætər] (v.) 使破滅
14. **lose one's temper** 發脾氣
15. **smash** [ˋsmæʃ] (v.) 打碎

## Chapter One

# A Mysterious[1] Stranger

In the darkness of a February night, a stranger dressed in a wide-brimmed[2] hat and very long coat got off a train at Bramblehurst. It was bitterly[3] cold, but there were no carriages[4]. The man had to carry his suitcase for several hours through a snow-storm to reach the small town of Iping. When he arrived, he went to the Coach[5] and Horses Inn. The people in the inn saw a dark figure[6] stumble[7] in.

"I want a room and a fire. Quickly, please!" the stranger demanded[8].

---

1. **mysterious** [mɪ`stɪriəs] (a.) 神祕的
2. **wide-brimmed** 闊緣的;寬邊的
3. **bitterly** [`bɪtəli] (adv.) 非常地
4. **carriage** [`kerɪdʒ] (n.) 四輪馬車
5. **coach** [koutʃ] (n.) 四輪大馬車;公共馬車
6. **figure** [`fɪjur] (n.) 人影
7. **stumble** [`stʌmbl̩] (v.) 跟蹌;蹣跚而行
8. **demand** [dɪ`mænd] (v.) 要求
9. **snap** [snæp] (v.) 厲聲說

The owner of the inn said, "I'm Mrs. Hall. Please come this way."

The woman showed the stranger to his room.

She left and soon returned with some food. The room was very warm now, but the man was still wearing his hat, coat and gloves.

"I can take your coat for you," Mrs. Hall said.

"No!" snapped[9] the stranger.

"Alright." said the woman as she left the room.

One Point Lesson

◆ A stranger **dressed in** a wide-brimmed hat and very long coat got off a train at Bramblehurst.
一名陌生人穿戴著闊邊帽和一件很長的大衣,他在布蘭堡赫斯特的火車站下車。

**dressed in**:穿戴著(衣物)。

15

In the kitchen, Mrs. Hall realized she had forgotten the mustard[1], so she took it up to the man. She knocked on the door and opened it. She stood in the doorway[2], stunned[3]. The strange man had large bulky[4] bandages[5] around his head. All she could see were his blue glasses, a shiny pink nose and some hair poking[6] through the bandages.

"I . . . I will take your things now, sir," she stammered[7].

"Leave the hat," he demanded.

Mrs. Hall noticed that the stranger was still wearing his gloves and he was holding a napkin over his face. He was wearing a dark dressing gown[8] of which he had the collar[9] turned up[10] high. Around his neck, he had tied a scarf. Every part of his body was completely covered.

"Y . . . y . . . yes, sir," said the shocked Mrs. Hall.

"He must have had a terrible accident," Mrs. Hall thought.

---

1. **mustard** [ˋmʌstərd] (n.) 芥末
2. **doorway** [ˋdɔːrweɪ] (n.) 門口
3. **stun** [stʌn] (v.) 使大吃一驚；使目瞪口呆
4. **bulky** [ˋbʌlki] (a.) 笨重的
5. **bandage** [ˋbændɪdʒ] (n.) 繃帶
6. **poke** [poʊk] (v.) 突出；伸出
7. **stammer** [ˋstæmər] (v.) 結結巴巴地說
8. **dressing gown** 浴袍
9. **collar** [ˋkɑːlər] (n.) 衣領
10. **turn up** 朝上
11. **tray** [treɪ] (n.) 托盤
12. **mood** [muːd] (n.) 心情；情緒
13. **baggage** [ˋbægɪdʒ] (n.) 行李

Some time later, she returned for the tray[11]. After eating and becoming warm, the stranger's mood[12] had much improved and he now said, "I left some baggage[13] at Bramblehurst Station, Mrs. Hall. Is there some way to bring it here?"

One Point Lesson

1. He was wearing a dark dressing gown **of which** he had the collar turned up high.
   他穿著一件深色的浴袍，浴袍的領子被往上拉高。
   → 句中 of which 的 which 為關係代名詞，指涉 dressing gown。

2. He **must have** had a terrible accident.
   他一定遭遇過可怕的意外。
   → **must have + 過去分詞**：推斷過去曾經發生過某事。

    "The roads are bad tonight, so my husband will get it for you in the morning. It is too easy to have an accident in all this snow," she replied.

    "Yes, an accident. I, too, had an accident."

    "What kind of acci-?" Mrs. Hall started to ask.

    "Never mind[1] about that," said the stranger. "You only need to know that I am a scientist, and all of my equipment[2] is in my bags. I need them all as soon as possible. I'm working on[3] a very important experiment[4]."

    Mrs. Hall left and thought, "He is a mysterious man."

She quickly returned to the bar[5] to tell her customers[6] about the mysterious man. One customer, Teddy Henfrey, said, "Hah! I bet he's hiding from the police. He hasn't had any accident!"

"Who's hiding from the police?" said a voice behind them. It was Mr. Hall.

"A stranger who just arrived tonight. He has bags at the station. You should take a good look[7] at them in the morning," warned Teddy.

"Cut it out[8] now all of you," snapped Mrs. Hall. "You'll all mind your own business."

But Mrs. Hall was very suspicious[9] of the stranger.

1. **mind** [maɪnd] (v.) 介意;注意
2. **equipment** [ɪˋkwɪpmənt] (n.) 設備;用具
3. **work on** 進行（計畫等）
4. **experiment** [ɪkˋspɛrɪmənt] (n.) 實驗
5. **bar** [bɑːr] (n.) 酒吧;酒館
6. **customer** [ˋkʌstəmər] (n.) 顧客
7. **take a good look** 仔細看看
8. **cut it out** 別再說了;停止
9. **suspicious** [səˋspɪʃəs] (a.) 猜疑的;起疑心的

One Point Lesson

I bet he's hiding from the police.
我敢打賭他一定是在躲警察。

I bet (that) . . . :表示篤定的說法。

The next morning, Mr. Hall brought the mysterious man's luggage[1] to the inn.

"Good grief[2]!" exclaimed[3] Mrs. Hall. "How many boxes and bags does he have?"

The stranger came out and started to help unload[4] the cart[5]. At that moment, a dog came growling[6] at the strange man and then bit his leg. Looking at his torn[7] clothes, the man quickly went back to his room.

"I'll go and see if he is alright," Mr. Hall said. He went in and found the man's door open. He was about to speak when he saw the most startling[8] thing. The man's coat arm was waving around in the air but there was no hand! Suddenly, Mr. Hall felt himself being violently[9] pushed out of the room. Then, there was a loud, BANG[10]! The door slammed shut[11].

Mr. Hall was confused.

"Did I see what I think I saw?" he asked himself.

By now, a small crowd had gathered and everyone

---

1. **luggage** [ˋlʌgɪdʒ] (n.) 行李
2. **Good grief!** 我的天啊！
   （表示驚訝的說法）
3. **exclaim** [ɪkˋskleɪm] (v.) 驚呼
4. **unload** [ʌnˋlod] (v.)
   從……卸下貨物
5. **cart** [kɑːrt] (n.)
   （馬、牛等拉的）運貨車
6. **growl** [graʊl] (v.) （狗等）嗥叫
7. **torn** [ter] (a.)
   被撕裂的；被扯破的
8. **startling** [ˋstɑːrtlɪŋ] (a.)
   令人吃驚的
9. **violently** [ˋvaɪələntli] (adv.)
   粗暴地
10. **bang** [bæŋ] (n.) 砰的聲音
11. **slam shut** 猛然關上
12. **reappear** [ˋriːəˋpɪr] (v.)
    再出現

was talking about the dog attack. "He needs to have the bite looked at," said someone in the crowd. "Well, I didn't see any blood," said another. The stranger now reappeared[12] wearing new clothes.

"Are you hurt, sir?" asked Mrs. Hall.

"Not at all," he replied.

---

One Point Lesson

1. He **was about to** speak when he saw the most startling thing.
   他正要說話時，看到了一件驚人的事情。
   → **be about to**：表示「即將做某件事」。

2. Suddenly, Mr. Hall felt himself **being** violently **pushed** out of the room. 突然間，霍爾先生感覺到自己被粗暴地推出房間。
   → **being + 過去式**：「正在被……」，表示進行中的被動態。

Eventually[1], all of the man's luggage was taken to his room. He quickly unpacked[2] his equipment and started to work. He worked all morning and at lunch time Mrs. Hall brought him his lunch. She knocked on the door, but he didn't answer, so she just went in. However, he wasn't wearing his glasses, and his eye sockets[3] were empty.

"My Lord![4]" she gasped[5].

The man, hearing her gasp, quickly put on his glasses. "You shouldn't come in without knocking," he said angrily.

"But I did knock." she said.

"You mustn't disturb[6] me. I have to concentrate[7]."

"Very well, Sir," Mrs. Hall replied. "There is a lock on the door. I suggest[8] you use it."

Then Mrs. Hall left.

---

1. **eventually** [ɪˋventjuəli] (adv.) 終於;最後
2. **unpack** [ʌnˋpæk] (v.) 從(箱、包中)取出
3. **socket** [ˋsɑːkɪt] (n.) (人體的)窩
4. **My Lord!** 我的天啊! (表驚嘆之意)
5. **gasp** [gæsp] (v.) 倒抽一口氣
6. **disturb** [dɪˋstɜːb] (v.) 打擾
7. **concentrate** [ˋkɑːnsəntreɪt] (v.) 專注
8. **suggest** [səˋdʒest] (v.) 建議
9. **footstep** [ˋfʊtstep] (n.) 腳步聲
10. **patience** [ˋpeɪʃəns] (n.) 耐心

For the rest of the afternoon, the man worked silently in his room. Suddenly, however, Mrs. Hall heard the sound of smashing bottles and heavy footsteps[9]. She quickly went upstairs. She was too afraid to knock, so she just listened.

"This is impossible!" she heard the man say. "I will never finish this experiment like this. It will take forever! I don't have the patience[10]!"

✔️ *Check Up* True or False.

Ⓣ Ⓕ ⓐ The man worked all morning and afternoon.

Ⓣ Ⓕ ⓑ Mrs. Hall heard the sound of smashing bottles and came into the man's room.

Ans: a. T  b. F

One Point Lesson

◆ You shouldn't come in **without knocking**.
你不該沒敲門就進來。

**without + V-ing**：沒有（做某動作）。

🎧 6

For a number of weeks, the stranger worked in his room. He was usually quiet, but there was the occasional[1] tantrum[2] when he smashed furniture and his equipment. Rarely, he took walks in the early evening. He always kept himself covered and ignored the friendly gestures from the village people. Mr. Hall proposed[3] that they get rid of[4] the stranger but Mrs. Hall said, "He always pays his bills plus extra[5]. We cannot be picky[6] when we have so many empty rooms."

---

1. **occasional** [əˋkeɪʒnəl] (a.) 偶爾的
2. **tantrum** [ˋtæntrəm] (n.) 發脾氣
3. **propose** [prəˋpouz] (v.) 提議
4. **get rid of** 擺脫
5. **extra** [ˋekstrə] (n.) 附加費用
6. **picky** [ˋpɪki] (a.) 挑剔的
7. **donation** [douˋneɪʃən] (n.) 捐款；捐贈
8. **fund** [fʌnd] (n.) 基金
9. **meanwhile** [ˋmiːnwaɪl] (adv.) 同時

The stranger was a very common topic of conversation among the village people. Many believed Teddy Henfrey's story that the man was running from the law.

One man was particularly curious about the stranger. He was the village doctor, John Cuss. He heard all about the thousands of bottles and wanted to see them. One day, he found a good reason to visit the stranger. He would ask for a donation[7] to the Nurse's Fund[8]. Mrs. Hall took him to the stranger's room. Dr. Cuss knocked and entered the room. Meanwhile[9], Mrs. Hall waited outside. About ten minutes later, there was a loud sound of stomping[10], some laughter and then the door was quickly flung open[11]. Dr. Cuss, with a face white with terror[12], went running out of the room. The eerie[13] sound of the stranger's laughter could be heard behind him.

10. **stomp** [stɑ:mp] (v.)
    踩腳；重踩
11. **fling a door open**
    用力將門甩開
    (fling-flung-flung)

12. **terror** [`terər] (n.) 驚恐
13. **eerie** [`ɪri] (a.)
    令人毛骨悚然的；怪異的

✔ *Check Up* Choose the correct answer.

Many of the village people believed that the man was a _____.

ⓐ policeman    ⓑ criminal    ⓒ doctor

Ans: b

Dr. Cuss fled[1] from the inn and ran straight to the Reverend[2] Bunting's home. He rushed in to see a bewildered[3] Reverend.

"I'm going crazy!" he exclaimed.

"What are you talking about?" asked the Reverend.

"The stranger! I went to see him to ask for a donation. I went into his room and he was sitting in a chair with his hands in his pockets. I asked him, 'Are you working on a secret research project?' He just snapped at me. 'Yes. I've been working on it for years. My most important notes were written on some sheets of paper.' Then some wind blew and they flew up the chimney. He took his hands out of his pockets and pretended to grab at[4] the flying papers. But there were no hands in his sleeves[5].

I asked him, 'Where are your hands?' He got up and came toward me. It was so creepy[6]! He put his face right next to mine. He lifted his arm up and I could see an empty sleeve coming toward

1. **flee** [fliː] (v.) 逃走
   (flee-fled-fled)
2. **reverend** [`rɛvərənd] (n.) 教士
3. **bewildered** [bɪ`wɪldərd] (a.)
   困惑的
4. **grab at** 抓
5. **sleeve** [sliːv] (n.) 衣袖
6. **creepy** [`kriːpi] (a.)
   令人毛骨悚然的
7. **pinch** [pɪnʃ] (v.) 捏

my face. Next thing I knew, it felt like a finger and a thumb had pinched[7] my nose!"

Now the Reverend started laughing. "Have you been drinking, Cuss?" he asked the doctor.

"No! No! You must believe me. I even swung my arm to hit his empty sleeve. It felt like I was hitting an arm. I'm telling you the truth! He was just like a ghost!"

**✓ Check Up** Choose the correct answer.

ⓐ Dr. Cuss threw the sheets of paper into the chimney.

ⓑ Dr. Cuss saw a ghost.

ⓒ The reverend didn't believe Dr. Cuss.

Ans: c

**One Point Lesson**

• It felt like a finger and a thumb had pinched my nose!
感覺上像是有根手指和拇指捏了我的鼻子！

it felt like . . . : 「感覺上像是……」，用來描述主觀的感覺。

**A** Choose the correct answer.

**❶** The stranger was holding a napkin _____ his face.

(a) for          (b) over          (c) under

**❷** I'm working _____ a very important experiment.

(a) at          (b) on          (c) through

**❸** Mr. Hall felt himself being violently pushed _____ the room.

(a) out of          (b) up          (c) behind

**❹** Mrs. Hall heard the sound _____ smashing bottles.

(a) at          (b) to          (c) of

**B** Choose the correct answer.

**❶** Mrs. Hall was very _____ of the stranger.

(a) mysterious    (b) suspicious    (c) confused

**❷** The stranger started to help _____ the cart.

(a) unpack          (b) reappear          (c) unload

**❸** You mustn't _____ me. I have to concentrate.

(a) disturb          (b) ignore          (c) smash

**C** Rearrange the sentences in chronological order.

**1** A dog jumped at the strange man's leg.

**2** Dr. Cuss went to the stranger to ask for a donation.

**3** A stranger arrived at the inn and asked for a room.

**4** The strange man's luggage arrived at the inn.

**5** Mrs. Hall saw the man's eye sockets were empty.

\_\_\_\_\_ ⇨ \_\_\_\_\_ ⇨ \_\_\_\_\_ ⇨ \_\_\_\_\_ ⇨ \_\_\_\_\_

**D** Fill in the blanks with the given words.

equipment   picky   rid   occasional   covered

For a number of weeks, the stranger worked in his room. He was usually quiet, but there was the **1**_____ tantrum when he smashed furniture and his **2**_____. He always kept himself **3**_____ and ignored the friendly gestures from the village people. Mr. Hall proposed that they get **4**_____ of the stranger but Mrs. Hall said, "He always pays his bills plus extra. We cannot be **5**_____ when we have so many empty rooms."

## Chapter Two

# A Puzzling[1] Robbery[2]

About a month passed when one morning in May, Mrs. Bunting heard noises outside her bedroom window.

"Wake up! Wake up!" she whispered to her sleeping husband, the Reverend. "Someone's in the house!"

He got up, took a poker[3] from the fireplace and crept[4] out into the hallway[5]. He heard the sound of sneezing[6] downstairs. The Reverend and Mrs. Bunting slowly made their way[7] down the stairs. They heard the sound of paper rustling[8] in the study.

---

1. **puzzling** [`pʌzlɪŋ] (a.) 令人困惑的
2. **robbery** [`rɑːbəri] (n.) 搶案
3. **poker** [`poukər] (n.) 火鉗
4. **creep** [kriːp] (v.) 悄悄行進 (creep-crept-crept)
5. **hallway** [`hɑːlweɪ] (n.) 走廊
6. **sneeze** [sniːz] (v.) 打噴嚏
7. **make one's way** (+prep.) 前進
8. **rustle** [`rʌsəl] (v.) 沙沙作響
9. **peer in** 往內瞧
10. **burglar** [`bɜːglər] (n.) 破門盜竊者
11. **clink** [klɪŋk] (n.) 叮噹聲

They came to the door and peered in[9]. What should have been a dark room was now lit by a candle. In the light, they could see that one of the drawers had been opened, but there was no sign of a burglar[10] in the room. Suddenly, there was a sound. Clink[11]! Clink!

"He has found our money," Mrs. Bunting whispered. "It's more than two thousand pounds!"

**One Point Lesson**

1. They **heard** the sound of paper **rustling** in the study.
   他們聽到書房裡傳來紙張沙沙作響的聲音。

   → **hear/see + A + V-ing**：聽到 A 發出的某種聲音。

2. What **should have been** a dark room was now lit by a candle. 本來應該是黑暗的房間，現在被蠟燭點亮了。

   → **should have + V-pp**：過去應該，表示「與現在事實相反」。

   e.g You **should have** not lied to me. 你那時不該對我說謊的。

🎧 9

The Reverend was very angry now. He rushed in and yelled, "I've caught you! Surrender yourself[1]!"

Mrs. Bunting rushed in behind her husband. Both of them were completely dumb-founded[2].

"But the room is empty!" the Reverend cried.

"Listen!" exclaimed his wife. "There is someone here. I can hear breathing[3]."

1. **surrender oneself**
   投降;自首
2. **dumb-founded**
   (受到驚嚇而)啞口無言的
3. **breathe** [briːð] (v.) 呼吸
4. **search** [sɜːtʃ] (v.) 搜索
5. **definitely** [ˋdefɪnətli] (adv.)
   絕對;必然
6. **be gone** 不在了
7. **front door** 前門

They searched[4] the room but could find no one.

"Someone was definitely[5] here. The lamp is lit, and our money is gone[6]."

"Ah-choo!" The sound of someone sneezing came from the hall, and the Buntings ran out to see who was there. They rushed into the hallway only to hear the kitchen door slam. They ran and flung it open but saw no one.

It was not long after the burglary when the Halls got up and found that the front door[7] of their inn was unlocked.

**One Point Lesson**

1. They rushed into the hallway **only to hear** the kitchen door slam.
   他們衝進走廊，卻只聽到廚房的門猛然關上的聲音。
   → **only to + V**：結果卻……

2. **It was not long after** the burglary **when** the Halls got up and found that . . .
   在竊盜案發生後不久，霍爾夫婦起床並發現……
   → **It was not long after . . . when . . .**：是在……之後不久時（發生了某事）。

"I know I locked the door last night," said Mrs. Hall.

"Who else would do this?" said Mr. Hall pointing to[1] the strange man's room.

They went up to the man's room. They knocked on the door but there was no reply.

"Let's go in." said Mrs. Hall. They opened the door and when they entered, they saw no one in the room. "It's empty but all of his clothes are here. And look at all of these bandages." commented[2] Mrs. Hall. "His bed is cold. That means he's been up[3] for a while."

At that moment, the strangest thing occurred[4]. All of the sheets bundled[5] themselves up together and then jumped over the bed. Then, the stranger's hat flew through the air and hit Mrs. Hall in the face. There was a terrible sound of a wicked[6] laugh. Next, they saw an armchair moving through the air toward them.

1. **point to** 指向
2. **comment** [ˋkɑːment] (v.) 發表意見
3. **up** [ʌp] (adv.) 起床；起來
4. **occur** [əˋkɜːr] (v.) 發生
5. **bundle** [ˋbʌndl̩] (v.) 捆
6. **wicked** [ˋwɪkɪd] (a.) 邪惡的
7. **scream** [skriːm] (v.) 尖叫；放聲大叫
8. **bolt** [boʊlt] (n.) 門栓
9. **deal with** 與……交易
10. **spirit** [ˋspɪrɪt] (n.) 靈魂
11. **explanation** [ˌekspləˋneɪʃən] (n.) 解釋

Mrs. Hall screamed[7] and felt herself being pushed out of the room with her husband in front of her. Then, the door slammed shut and the bolt[8] locked. Mrs. Hall said to her husband, "He deals with[9] the devil. He has evil spirits[10] in there."

"There has to be another explanation[11]," said her husband.

✓ *Check Up* Choose the correct answer.

The strange man has been gone without the _____.

 a notice          b knock          c bandages

Ans: c

One Point Lesson

• The stranger's hat flew through the air and **hit** Mrs. Hall **in the face**.
陌生人的帽子騰空飛過來，打中霍爾太太的臉。

--------------------------------------------------

**hit + A + in the (face, arm, etc.)**：打中 A 的（身體部位）。

35

"I want him out of my inn. He's put evil spirits in the furniture," said Mrs. Hall.

Suddenly, they heard a noise at the top of the stairs.

"Stay out of my room. You have no right[1] to go in there," the stranger shouted at them. Now the Halls stared at[2] each other. "How is that possible? We were just there. He wasn't. How could he. . . ?" Mrs. Hall gasped.

But for the rest of the morning, they did not see him. In fact, they even ignored the bell when he rang.

By noon, everyone had heard about the burglary at the Buntings' house. All the regulars[3] were at the bar, gossiping[4] about the robbery. It was quite noisy when the conversation suddenly halted[5].

The stranger had entered the bar and demanded, "Why didn't you bring me my breakfast and why didn't you answer the bell?"

"You haven't paid your bill. No money, so no food or room," Mrs. Hall replied angrily.

"I told you I would give it to you in a few days. Here it is now."

"Well, that's interesting. How did you get it? And you have to explain what you did to my furniture and how you got in your room without coming through the door," she demanded.

1. **right** [raɪt] (n.) 權利
2. **stare at** 盯著……看
3. **regular** [ˋrɛgjulər] (n.) 老顧客
4. **gossip** [ˋgɑːsəp] (v.) 閒聊；傳播流言
5. **halt** [hɑːlt] (v.) 停止

**One Point Lesson**

Explain **what** you did to my furniture and **how** you got in your room without coming through the door. 解釋你對我的家具做了什麼，還有你怎麼能不經過門就進到自己的房間。

what / how+S+V：（某人）做了什麼／如何做到某事。

**Check Up** Choose the correct answer.

Mrs. Hall didn't understand _____.

a how the man entered his room
b how the man rang the bell
c how the man got the money

Ans: a

37

This made the man very angry. "Stop this! You have no idea[1] about me," he shouted. "Very well then, I'll show you." The man put his hand to his face. He put a small rubbery[2] thing in her hand.

"Look! It's his nose. He has a hole in his face," everyone screamed. Then the man tore off[3] his glasses and everything on his face. Suddenly, the man dressed in a long coat had no head. Everyone became hysterical[4] and ran out of the inn. No one had been prepared to see such a thing.

Mrs. Hall said, "He is an evil spirit."

A policeman who had heard all the commotion[5] came and asked, "What on earth[6] is going on here?"

"A headless[7] man is inside the inn," Mr. Hall told him. "Very well," said the policeman. "I will go and arrest[8] him."

---

1. **have no idea** 不了解；不知道
2. **rubbery** [ˋrʌbəri] (a.) 橡膠似的
3. **tear off** 扯下；撕下
4. **hysterical** [hɪˋstɛrɪkəl] (a.) 歇斯底里的；情緒失控的
5. **commotion** [kəˋmoʊʃən] (n.) 騷動；混亂
6. **on earth** 到底
7. **headless** [ˋhɛdləs] (a.) 無頭的
8. **arrest** [əˋrɛst] (v.) 逮捕

> **One Point Lesson**
>
> ◆ A policeman who **had heard** all the commotion came . . .
> 一位聽到了這陣騷動的警察過來……
>
> ----
>
> **had + V-pp**：過去完成式（在過去式的句子中，表示此事在之前已經發生過）

Mr. Hall and the policeman went into the inn. The innkeeper pointed at a headless body and said, "There he is."

The stranger now asked angrily, "What do you think you are doing?"

✔ *Check Up* Fill in the blanks with proper word.

When the man tore off everything on his face, he became _____.

Ans: headless

One Point Lesson

**What do you** think you are doing? 你以為你在做什麼？

What are you doing?（你在做什麼？）和 Do you think?
（你覺得？）兩種句法結合，成為以 do you think 為核心的問句，
而 are you doing 作為 think 的補語，要還原成直述句的順序，
變成 you are doing。

**What do you think** the problem is? 你覺得問題是什麼？

39

The policeman said, "I must arrest you."

"Keep away[1] from me," the stranger cautioned[2].

The policeman moved toward the stranger. The stranger now removed[3] one of his gloves and hit the policeman with his fist[4].

"Grab his legs!" shouted the policeman. Mr. Hall tried to grab his legs but the stranger hit him hard. The policeman finally managed to[5] push the stranger to the ground.

"I give up." said the stranger. He stood up and quickly started to remove his clothes. The two men saw a clothed body bending[6] over to remove shoes that had no feet.

Mr. Hall exclaimed, "That's not a man. There's nothing inside the shirt." He put his hand out to see if[7] he could touch the man, but then there was a loud shriek[8], "OWWW! That's my eye. I am a man. I'm just invisible[9]. But that doesn't give you the right to arrest or poke[10] me in the eye."

1. **keep away** 遠離
2. **caution** [ˋkɔːʃən] (v.) 警告
3. **remove** [rɪˋmuːv] (v.) 脫掉
4. **fist** [fɪst] (n.) 拳頭
5. **manage to** 設法做到
6. **bend** [bɛnd] (v.) 彎腰 (bend-bent-bent)
7. **see if** 看看是否……
8. **shriek** [ʃriːk] (v.) 尖聲叫
9. **invisible** [ɪnˋvɪzɪbl̩] (a.) 隱形的；看不到的
10. **poke** [poʊk] (v.) 戳
11. **trousers** [ˋtraʊzərz] (n.) 褲子

Then the policeman said, "I'm arresting you for the burglary of the Buntings' house." But by now, the man had removed his shoes, socks and trousers[11]. All they could see was a shirt running around the room.

*Check Up* Fill in the blanks with proper word.

The man was _____, so nobody could see him.

Ans: invisible

One Point Lesson

- But that doesn't **give you the right to arrest** or poke me in the eye. 但那並不代表你就有權利逮捕我，或戳我的眼睛。

**give A the right to + V**：給某人權利做某事。

Just outside of Iping, a tramp[1], Thomas Marvel, sat looking at two pairs of[2] shoes, trying to decide which pair to wear. He was studying[3] the boots intently[4] when a voice behind him said, "Both of them are very ugly."

"Yes," said the tramp. "Which ones should I wear?" Then, he turned his head to ask, "What are you wearing?"

But as he finished his question, he saw no one was there. "I am mad," he said aloud.

"No, you're not," said the voice behind him.

"Where are you?" asked the tramp. I must be drunk[5] or just talking to myself."

1. **tramp** [træmp] (n.) 流浪漢
2. **pair of** 一對
3. **study** [ˋstʌdi] (v.) 細看
4. **intently** [ɪnˋtentli] (adv.) 專注地
5. **drunk** [drʌŋk] (a.) 喝醉的
6. **shake** [ʃeɪk] (v.) 搖
7. **imagine** [ɪˋmædʒɪn] (v.) 想像
8. **idiot** [ˋɪdɪət] (n.) 笨蛋

One Point Lesson

Thomas Marvel, sat looking at two pairs of shoes, trying to decide **which** pair **to wear**. 湯瑪斯・馬佛，一邊坐著，一邊看著兩雙鞋子，想決定要穿哪一雙鞋。

which + N + to V：要選擇哪一個來……

"No, don't worry. You are not drunk."

The tramp looked around again, feeling very confused. "I'm sure I heard a voice."

Just then, something grabbed Marvel by the collar and shook[6] him.

"You're not imagining[7] anything," said the voice. "I am an invisible man."

Marvel then said, "I am a tramp, but I'm not an idiot[8]. No one can be invisible."

Check Up  Answer the question.

Why did the tramp feel confused?

_____

Ans: Because he couldn't see the invisible man but heard his voice.

At that moment, the tramp felt something grab his hand, and he jumped back. Then, Marvel put out his hand to feel the hand that had grabbed his. He then felt an arm, a chest[1], then a beard.

"This is truly amazing[2]," said the tramp. "How is this possible?"

"I will tell you later," said the invisible man. "Now, I need your help. Society has rejected both of us. So, we should try to help each other."

"How could I help you?" asked Marvel.

"First with clothes and shelter[3]. I can also help you. Can you imagine what power I have? If you betray[4] me, I could do terrible things."

---

1. **chest** [tʃest] (n.) 胸膛
2. **amazing** [əˋmeɪzɪŋ] (a.) 驚人的
3. **shelter** [ˋʃeltər] (n.) 棲身處
4. **betray** [bɪˋtreɪ] (v.) 背叛
5. **settle down** 平靜下來
6. **mixture** [ˋmɪkstʃə] (n.) 混合
7. **relief** [rɪˋliːf] (n.) 寬心；解脫

The tramp was very frightened now. "Alright. I . . . won't betray you," he stuttered. "Don't worry. I will help you."

Back in Iping, everything had settled down[5]. People felt a mixture[6] of doubt that the strange man had existed, and relief[7] that he was gone. At about four in the afternoon, however, a tramp entered the village and went straight to the strange man's room.

**One Point Lesson**

◆ First (help me) with clothes and shelter.
先從衣物和棲身處開始幫起。

---

**help A with + N**：幫助某人得到⋯⋯

45

The tramp saw two men, Dr. Cuss and Reverend Bunting, looking through[1] three large books.

"It's some kind of code[2]," said Dr. Cuss.

"What are you doing?" asked the tramp. The two men looked up but were relieved[3] to see a tramp.

"The bar is below," said the doctor.

"Thank you," replied Marvel. He went downstairs, had a drink and went out to wait below the invisible man's room.

1. **look through** 翻閱
2. **code** [koʊd] (n.) 密碼
3. **relieve** [rɪ`liːv] (v.) 使放心
4. **private** [`praɪvət] (a.) 私人的
5. **bundle** [`bʌndl̩] (n.) 捆

6. **punch** [pʌntʃ] (v.) 揍
7. **unconscious** [ʌn`kɑːnʃəs] (a.) 不省人事的

Back in the bedroom, the two men were looking through the books. Suddenly, they felt something cold and sharp against their necks.

"I don't want to hurt you, but you've given me no choice," said a familiar voice. "What gave you the right to look through my private[4] things? And where are my clothes?"

"Mrs. Hall took them."

"Well then, I'll just have to . . ."

"No!" screamed the doctor and the reverend. Minutes later, a bundle[5] of books flew out of the window. They were caught by the tramp. Mr. Huxter, a shop owner across the street, saw this and yelled out, "Stop! Thief!" He started to run after the tramp but felt himself punched[6] in the face. He fell to the ground unconscious[7].

☑ Check Up  Choose the correct answer.

Why did the invisible man go back to the inn?

a To pay the bill.

b To get his books back.

c To meet Dr. Cuss and the reverend.

Ans: b

One Point Lesson

They felt **something cold and sharp** against their necks. 他們感覺到有又冷又尖銳的東西頂在脖子上。

---

**something + 形容詞**：……的東西。

47

A few moments later, Dr. Cuss came running down the stairs of the inn. He shouted out, "He has my trousers and all of the reverend's clothing[1]. Stop him!"

Behind him, the reverend came running out, covering his body with a rug[2] and a daily newspaper. The two men went running down the street and tripped over[3] Mr. Huxter's unconscious body. Other people had come to see what the commotion was about. It was at that time that people were thrown to the ground or punched in the face. Terrified[4], everyone ran away[5].

However, the invisible man was very angry. He returned to the town and started to destroy[6] everything. With an ax[7], he chopped[8] Mr. Hall's cart to pieces. He went to Dr. Cuss's office and smashed everything. He threw street lamps through windows and cut the telegraph[9] wires[10].

1. **clothing** [`kloʊðɪŋ] (n.) 衣服
2. **rug** [rʌg] (n.) 毯子
3. **trip over** 被……絆倒
4. **terrified** [`terəfaɪd] (a.) 驚嚇的

5. **run away** 逃跑
6. **destroy** [dɪ`strɔɪ] (v.) 摧毀
7. **ax** [æks] (n.) 斧頭
8. **chop** [tʃɑːp] (v.) 劈；砍

One Point Lesson

It was at that time that people were thrown to the ground . . .
就在這個時候，人們被摔倒在地上……

It . . . that . . . :「就是……」，表強調語氣。

*The Invisible Man*

After the invisible man's rage [11] was over, he left Iping, and no one ever saw, heard or felt him ever again.

9. **telegraph** [`telɔgræf] (n.) 電信；電報

10. **wire** [waɪr] (n.) 電纜；電線

11. **rage** [reɪdʒ] (n.) 盛怒

✅ *Check Up* Choose the correct answer.

Which thing didn't the invisible man do when he got so angry?

a He destroyed Mr. Hall's cart.

b He cut the telegraph wires.

c He took Mr. Hall's clothes.

Ans: c

**One Point Lesson**

He chopped Mr. Hall's cart to pieces.
他將霍爾先生的手推車劈成碎片。

**to pieces**：變成碎片；支離破碎

49

**A** Read the four sentences and write down who said each sentence.

the invisible man    the tramp    Mr. Bunting    Mrs. Hall

**1** I've caught you. Surrender yourself. _____

**2** He deals with the devil. He has evil spirits in there. _____

**3** I must be drunk or just talking to myself. _____

**4** Can you imagine what power I have? _____

**B** Match.

**1** slam • • **a** A noise caused by paper rubbing together

**2** halt • • **b** To speak unclearly and without confidence

**3** rustle • • **c** To stop doing something

**4** stutter • • **d** To show extreme, uncontrollable fear

**5** hysterical • • **e** To shut noisily with great force

## C Choose the correct answer.

**1** How could the Buntings know that there was someone in the room?

(a) Because the room was lit by a candle.

(b) Because the front door was open.

(c) Because they heard someone run out of the room.

**2** What was revealed when the man tore off everything on his face?

(a) He had a terrible disease.

(b) He had no face.

(c) He turned into a ghost.

**3** The man was very angry. What did he do?

(a) He left Iping with his three books.

(b) He stole money from the reverend.

(c) He went to Dr. Cuss's office and smashed everything.

## D True or False.

T F **1** The invisible man was poked in the eye during the fight in the inn.

T F **2** The tramp was happy to help the invisible man.

T F **3** The invisible man had the tramp harm Dr. Cuss and the reverend.

# Themes[1] of Wells's Science Fictions[2]

H.G. Wells was a socialist[3] thinker[4], and he was also very interested in the wonders of scientific developments. One of his most famous novels, *The Time Machine*, explored[5] both of these themes.

In this novel, Wells invents a time machine and portrays[6] the natural evolution[7] of the capitalist[8] class structure. A society of human called the Eloi in the story represents[9] the rich upper class who have everything they need and lose interest in life. Wells probably didn't think the class like this would be actually existed, but he does raise some interesting ideas with his description of the Eloi society.

1. **theme** [θiːm] (n.) 主題
2. **science fiction** 科幻小說
3. **socialist** [ˋsəuʃəlɪst] (n.) 社會主義者
4. **thinker** [ˋθɪŋkər] (n.) 思想家
5. **explore** [ɪkˋsplɔːr] (v.) 探索
6. **portray** [pɔːrˋtreɪ] (v.) 描寫
7. **evolution** [ˌiːvəˋluːʃən] (n.) 進化

Many of Wells's novels are now called science fiction. The main reason for this was because the plots[10] of these books depended heavily on[11] the impact[12] of scientific discoveries. It is no coincidence[13] that Wells was so interested in science. The end of the 18th century saw great advances[14] in scientific knowledge. The process of industrialization was

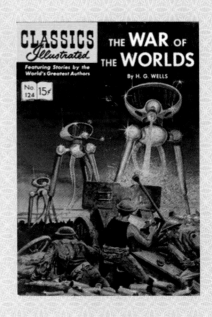

creating great changes in society. Many people wondered what the future would be like. Some saw a paradise[15], in which scientific progress would create a perfect society. Others saw human civilization descending into terrible ruin[16] as the rich took advantage of[17] the poor.

8. **capitalist** [ˋkæpɪtəlɪst] (a.) 資本家的

9. **represent** [ˏreprɪˋzent] (v.) 代表

10. **plot** [plɑːt] (n.) （小說、戲劇等的）情節

11. **depend on** 仰賴

12. **impact** [ˋɪmpækt] (n.) 衝擊

13. **coincidence** [koʊˋɪnsɪdəns] (n.) 巧合

14. **advance** [ədˋvɑːns] (n.) 進步；發展

15. **paradise** [ˋperədaɪs] (n.) 美好的地方；樂園

16. **ruin** [ˋruːɪn] (n.) 毀滅；廢墟

17. **take advantage of** 利用；佔⋯⋯的便宜

# · Chapter Three ·

## 🎧18 An Unwelcome¹ Visitor

**M**any, many miles from Iping, Thomas Marvel plodded² along a road, carrying three heavy books. He looked around, hoping to escape³. However, the invisible man always said to him, "If you escape, I'll find you, and I'll kill you."

"But I'm weak and can't help you," said the tramp.

"You had better do as I say. Everyone will be looking for me, and I need you to do the things I can't," said the invisible man. "You had better keep my books safe. If you don't, I will kill you."

---

1. **unwelcome** [ʌnˈwɛlkəm] (a.)
   不受歡迎的；不速之客的
2. **plod** [plɑːd] (v.)
   沉重緩慢地走
3. **escape** [ɪˈskeɪp] (v.) 逃跑
4. **pocket** [ˈpɑːkɪt] (v.)
   將……裝入口袋

---

✓*Check Up*  True or False.

T F  ⓐ The invisible man and the tramp borrowed money from the bank.

T F  ⓑ Thomas Marvel wanted to escape from the invisible man.

Ans: a. F  b. T

They walked for many hours and eventually arrived in Port Stowe in the morning. They waited until the bank opened. The invisible man went inside and Marvel waited outside. Suddenly, bundles of money came flying through the window which Marvel quickly pocketed[4] in his coat and trousers. He then ran until he was out of breath[5].

He found a seat and sat down with the three books next to him. Not long later, an old seaman[6] sat down next to him. He had a newspaper with him and said, "Look at this! It says there is an invisible man running around these parts[7]."

5. **out of breath** 喘不過氣來
6. **seaman** [`siːmən] (n.) 水手
7. **part** [pɑːrt] (n.) 地區；地方

**One Point Lesson**

1. You **had better** do as I say. 你最好照我說的去做。
   → **as**：依照；**had better**：最好

2. He . . . sat down **with** the three books next to him.
   他……坐下來，將三本書放在他身邊。
   → **with**：與……一起

55

🎧19

Marvel looked suspiciously[1] around himself. He listened carefully for any sound of the invisible man. He didn't hear anything, so he whispered to the seaman, "I know some things about the invisible man."

The seaman was astonished[2] and asked, "Really! What do you know?"

1. **suspiciously** [səˋspɪʃəsli] (adv.) 懷疑地
2. **astonished** [əˋstɑːnɪʃt] (a.) 吃驚的
3. **moan** [moʊn] (v.) 呻吟
4. **smack** [smæk] (v.) 摑掌
5. **make up** 編造；杜撰
6. **drag** [dræg] (v.) 拖
7. **head** [hed] (v.) 前往
8. **distance** [ˋdɪstəns] (n.) 距離
9. **microscope** [ˋmaɪkrəskoʊp] (n.) 顯微鏡

"Well, I . . . OWWW," moaned[3] the tramp. He now held his hand next to his left ear. The invisible man had smacked[4] him on the side of his head. "It's . . . uh . . . it's my . . . uh . . . tooth. Terrible toothache. I'm going now."

"What about the invisible man?" the seaman called out behind the tramp.

"It's not true. Some man I know made up[5] the whole story," said the tramp as he was dragged[6] along the road by the invisible man.

Marvel and the invisible man left Port Stowe and headed[7] toward Port Burdock which was a very short distance[8] away. In this town, Dr. Arthur Kemp, was looking through a microscope[9] in his study. He was a research scientist.

✔️ *Check Up* Which statement is true?

  a  The tramp told the seaman everything about the invisible man.
  b  The invisible man and the tramp went to meet Dr. Kemp.
  c  The tramp was smacked and he knew the invisible man was near to him.

Ans: c

Dr. Kemp decided to take a break[1], so he stood up and walked to the window. Through the window, he saw a dirty-looking[2] man running through the street, waving his arms. "Another crazy idiot screaming about the invisible man. Why does this town have so many?" he asked himself.

But the people who saw Marvel up close did not think he was crazy, especially[3] when they heard heavy breathing behind Marvel. Two boys were suddenly pushed to the ground and a dog was kicked by an invisible leg.

Everyone panicked[4] and deserted[5] the streets. Some even screamed as they ran, "The invisible man is here!" However, everything was normal[6] at the Jolly Cricketer Inn. The regulars were enjoying their regular brew[7] when Marvel came crashing[8] through the door, screaming, "The invisible man is after me. Lock the doors. He promised he would kill me if I escaped."

1. **take a break** 休息
2. **dirty-looking** 看起來很髒的
3. **especially** [ɪˋspeʃəli] (adv.) 尤其
4. **panic** [ˋpænɪk] (v.) 恐慌 (panic-panicked-panicked)
5. **desert** [dɪˋzɝːt] (v.) 遺棄
6. **normal** [ˋnɔːrməl] (a.) 正常的
7. **brew** [bruː] (n.) 酒
8. **crash** [kræʃ] (v.) 闖；衝
9. **bolt** [boʊlt] (v.) 栓住（門）
10. **thump** [θʌmp] (v.) 重擊
11. **in terror** 驚恐地
12. **barman** [ˋbɑːrmən] (n.) 酒保

A policeman said, "Hurry! Lock the doors!"

No sooner had they bolted[9] the door when a powerful thumping[10] was heard on the door.

"Don't open it," Marvel cried in terror[11]. "Are all of the doors locked?"

"The back door! The yard door!" exclaimed the barman[12].

<br>

One Point Lesson

• **No sooner** had they bolted the door **when** a powerful thumping was heard on the door.
他們才閂上門，就聽到門上傳來一聲強力的撞擊聲。

**No sooner + 倒裝句 + when (than)** .... : 一……就……

## 21

The barman rushed to check the doors, but it was too late. "The yard door is open. He could be inside now," he told them. Then, there was the sound of a slamming door. The barman reached for a knife, and the policeman for his gun. From nowhere[1], something dragged Marvel out from his hiding place.

The invisible man dragged Marvel into the kitchen. The policeman followed and tried to grab onto the invisible man, but he felt a large fist smash into his face. The barman and the policeman both

1. **nowhere** [`nouwer] (n.)
   不知名的地方；不存在之處
2. **tackle** [`tækl̩] (v.) 抓獲
3. **crawl** [krɑːl] (v.) 爬
4. **direction** [dɪ`rekʃən] (n.) 方向

tried to tackle[2] the man. While the invisible man was fighting off the two men, Marvel managed to crawl[3] away and escape through the yard door with the three books.

The fight continued for a few more moments. Then, the two men realized they could no longer feel the invisible man.

"Where is he?" one asked.

"He must have escaped," the other said.

Just then, a plate went flying through the air. The policeman shot five times in the direction[4] from which it came.

"You might have got him. Let's try to feel around for his body."

✔️ *Check Up* Fill in the blanks with proper word.

While the invisible man was fighting with the two men, Thomas Marvel _____.

Ans: escaped

One Point Lesson

You **might have got** him. 你可能射到他了。

**might have + V-pp**：可能已經……

## 22

In another part of town, Dr. Kemp was busily working on his research. He was taking down[1] some notes at the time of the fight. When he heard the gunshots[2], he lifted his head and thought, "Hmm. Another fight at the Cricketer tonight."

He went back to his work, but then the doorbell rang. After a few moments, no one came into his study to see him, so he called his housekeeper[3].

"Who was at the door?" he asked.

"No one," she told him. "It must have been a prank[4]."

Dr. Kemp then forgot about it and continued to work until two in the morning. He decided to go to bed so he went up to his room.

Just before he entered his room, he saw something that looked like blood on the floor. Then, he looked at the door handle and saw it covered with mud. He walked into his bedroom and saw blood all over the bed covers. Then, he looked closely[5] at his pillow. "Good Lord! It looks like someone was lying there," he cried.

1. **take down** 寫下
2. **gunshot** [ˈɡʌnʃɑːt] (n.) 槍聲
3. **housekeeper** [ˈhaʊsˌkiːpər] (n.) 女管家
4. **prank** [præŋk] (n.) 惡作劇
5. **closely** [ˈkloʊsli] (adv.) 仔細地
6. **stain** [steɪn] (v.) 沾污；弄髒

At that moment, there was another voice in the room. "Kemp! It's you. I don't believe it!"

Dr. Kemp looked around the room. In the corner, he saw what looked like a blood-stained[6] bandage wrapped around an arm that wasn't there.

*✓ Check Up*   Choose the correct answer.

Where was the invisible man now?

- a) At the door.
- b) In the study.
- c) In the bedroom.

Ans: c

## 23

"Don't worry, Kemp. I'm an invisible man. You aren't hearing things."

"What! An invisible man? So it's true what they've been saying in the village!" Dr. Kemp said, reaching out his hand to touch the bandage. But the invisible man grabbed the doctor's wrist[1]. Dr. Kemp tried to pull away[2] and fight, but the invisible man said, "Kemp! Stop this. You know me. I'm Jack Griffin. We went to college together."

1. **wrist** [rɪst] (n.) 手腕
2. **pull away** 抽身；甩開
3. **chemistry** [ˋkɛmɪstrɪ] (n.) 化學
4. **wounded** [ˋwuːndɪd] (a.) 受傷的
5. **exhausted** [ɪgˋzɑːst] (a.) 精疲力竭的
6. **pour** [pɔːr] (v.) 倒（液體）
7. **wardrobe** [ˋwɔːrdroʊb] (n.) 衣櫥
8. **robe** [roʊb] (n.) 浴袍；長袍
9. **underwear** [ˋʌndʒwɛr] (n.) 內衣；貼身衣物
10. **devour** [dɪˋvaʊr] (v.) 狼吞虎嚥地吃

Kemp now sat up and asked, "The Jack Griffin who won the college medal in chemistry[3] ?"

"Yes."

"Why would you want to make yourself invisible?" asked Dr. Kemp again. "And how?"

The invisible man replied, "Kemp, can I explain tomorrow? I'm wounded[4], exhausted[5], and hungry. Could I have something to drink?" Dr. Kemp poured[6] him some whiskey and asked, "Where are you?"

Griffin took the glass out of his hand. "I can't believe all of this is happening," said Dr. Kemp.

"I've been outside, running around with no clothes on. All I want is to put some clean clothes on and eat something." Dr. Kemp went to his wardrobe[7] and took out a dressing gown. "Will this be okay?"

The invisible man took the robe[8] and Dr. Kemp watched as it seemed to swing around in the air by itself. The doctor also got him some underwear[9], socks and slippers, and then went to get some food. He brought the food back, and watched as an invisible mouth devoured[10] it.

"This is the strangest thing," he muttered[1].

"What is strange is the good fortune[2] to enter the house of a man I know for bandages for my wound," Griffin said.

"How were you wounded?" asked the doctor.

"Well, there was a man who was supposed to[3] help me, Marvel."

"He shot[4] you?" the doctor questioned[5] him again.

"No, but he stole my books and money."

"Did you shoot him? I heard some shots coming from the inn."

"No, someone back at the inn shot me. But I'll explain later. I'm exhausted."

"Then sleep here in my room," offered the doctor.

"Sleep! I have to catch Marvel to get my books! And the police might catch me," said the man.

"Police?" asked Kemp.

"I'm such an idiot! I've given you the idea to turn me in[6]."

---

1. **mutter** [`mʌtər] (v.) 喃喃自語
2. **fortune** [`fɔːrtʃuːn] (n.) 運氣
3. **be supposed to** 應該要
4. **shoot** [ʃuːt] (v.) 開槍
   (shoot-shot-shot)
5. **question** [`kwestʃən] (v.) 詢問
6. **turn in** 密告;檢舉
7. **discover** [dɪ`skʌvər] (v.) 發現
8. **partner** [`pɑːrtnər] (n.) 伙伴
9. **capture** [`kæptʃər] (v.) 捕獲

"I promise I won't. I won't tell anyone that you are here. Why don't you lock the door after I leave?" Dr. Kemp suggested.

"Alright. Then I will sleep here tonight. I'll explain my plans to you tomorrow. There will be wonderful things that you and I can do together. I have just discovered[7] that if I am to be invisible, I must have a partner[8]."

The two men shook hands and said good-night but the invisible man warned, "You had better not think about trying to have me captured[9]."

One Point Lesson

If I **am to be** invisible, I must have a partner.
如果我要隱形，我必須有個伙伴。

**be to** + 原形動詞：表示「意圖做某事」。

67

Match the two parts of each sentence.

(a) when Marvel came crashing through the door

(b) but he felt a large fist smash into his face

(c) hoping to escape

(d) which Marvel pocketed in his coat and trousers

❶ Thomas Marvel looked around,

_____.

❷ Bundles of money came flying through the window

_____.

❸ The regulars were enjoying their regular brew

_____.

❹ The policeman tried to grab onto the invisible man,

_____.

B Choose the correct answer.

❶ Why did Dr. Kemp think that Thomas Marvel was crazy?

(a) Because the man looked very dirty.

(b) Because Kemp couldn't see the invisible man behind him.

(c) Because there were so many crazy people in the town.

❷ Why did the invisible man enter Dr. Kemp's home?

(a) Because he knew it was Dr. Kemp's home.

(b) Because he chose it randomly to get some bandages.

(c) Because they had planned to meet there.

**C** Fill in the blanks with the given words.

| voice | blood | covered | closely |
|---|---|---|---|

Just before he entered his room, he saw something that looked like ❶ _____ on the floor. Then he looked at the door handle and saw it was ❷ _____ with mud. He walked into his bedroom and saw blood all over the bed covers. Then, he looked ❸ _____ at his pillow. "Good Lord! It looks like someone was lying there," he cried. At that moment, there was another ❹ _____ in the room.

## Chapter Four

# A Wonderful Discovery[1]

Dr. Kemp left the room and heard the invisible man lock the door.

"I must be mad. None of this can be true," he thought to himself. "No! It is all true."

He quietly walked downstairs to his office and looked for the day's newspapers. He started to look for some articles[2]. The first he read was titled[3], "Strange Story from Iping." Another was named, "Entire Village in Sussex Goes Mad." He read stories of people being attacked, a doctor and a reverend being stripped[4] of their clothes and buildings being destroyed.

Dr. Kemp thought to himself, "This man is mad and dangerous. He is capable of[5] murder[6]."

---

1. **discovery** [dɪ`skʌvəri] (n.)
   發現
2. **article** [`ɑːrtɪkl] (n.)
   報導；文章
3. **title** [`taɪtl] (v.) 給……加標題
4. **strip** [strɪp] (v.) 脫去

5. **capable of** 能夠……的
6. **murder** [`mɜːdə] (n.)
   殺人；謀殺
7. **previous** [`priːvɪəs] (a.) 先前的
8. **concerned** [kən`sɜːnd] (a.)
   擔憂的

Dr. Kemp was very worried. He didn't sleep all
night, thinking about what he should do. In the
morning, his housekeeper came, and he asked
her to serve breakfast for two in his study. In his
office, he read the morning newspaper which
described the events of the previous[7] night. Dr.
Kemp, feeling even more concerned[8], sat down to
write a note. He addressed[9] it to "Colonel[10] Adye,
Port Burdock Police." Just as he was giving it to
his housekeeper, he heard the sound of
smashing furniture.

"Hurry." he whispered to his housekeeper.

9. **address** [əˋdrɛs] (v.)
（在信封上）寫上收件人
姓名、地址

10. **colonel** [ˋkɝnl] (n.)
陸軍上校

One Point Lesson

Dr. Kemp, feeling **even** more concerned . . .
凱普博士覺得更加擔心……

**even**：用來加強語氣。

Dr. Kemp rushed upstairs and knocked on the door. "What's the matter?" he asked the headless robe.

"I lost my temper," the invisible man explained.

"You seem to do that a lot. The papers are full of you. But no one knows that you are here."

The invisible man seemed very agitated[1], so Dr. Kemp suggested, "Why don't we have breakfast in my study?"

1. **agitated** [ˋædʒɪteɪtɪd] (a.) 激動的
2. **mood** [muːd] (n.) 心情
3. **nervously** [ˋnɜːvəsli] (adv.) 緊張地
4. **companion** [kəmˋpænjən] (n.) 同伴
5. **curious to** 好奇想……
6. **medicine** [ˋmedsən] (n.) 醫學
7. **physics** [ˋfɪzɪks] 物理學
8. **liquid** [ˋlɪkwɪd] (n.) 液體

This suggestion put Griffin in a better mood[2], and they went to the study. Dr. Kemp nervously[3] looked out the window and sat down across from his invisible companion[4].

"I'm curious to[5] know how all of this happened to you, Griffin," said Dr. Kemp.

"It was wonderful at first. But now, with all of the problems I've had, I'm not sure. Not unless great things can be done. Let me tell you my story," said Griffin. "As you know, we studied medicine[6] together many years ago. But did you know that later I changed to physics[7]? I studied a lot about light and liquids[8] and how glass becomes almost invisible in water when light goes through it."

✓ Check Up  Choose the correct answer.

Why did the invisible man smash the furniture?
ⓐ Because he got angry.
ⓑ Because his friend turned him in.
ⓒ Because he lost his money and books.

Ans: a

One Point Lesson

1. You seem to **do that** a lot. 你好像很常那麼做。
   → 句中的 do that 在這裡代表 lose your temper。

2. Not **unless** great things can be done.
   除非我能做到什麼一番大事。
   → **unless**：除非

## 27

"Yes, but humans aren't transparent[1] like glass," interrupted[2] Kemp.

"No, we are except for the red coloring of our blood and other matter[3]. Flesh[4], bone, nails, hair, everything is transparent. I did so much research for six years and wrote everything down in my three books. That's why I have to get them back from Marvel."

"But how did you get the blood and other pigment[5] to[6] become invisible?" Kemp asked.

"It took me three more years to do that. But I never had any money, so I stole it from my father. But then he shot himself because he actually owed the money I stole to[7] someone else. Well, with the money, I bought all of the equipment I needed. I started to be able to make things invisible.

---

1. **transparent** [træn`sperənt] (a.) 透明的
2. **interrupt** [͵ɪntə`rʌpt] (v.) 打斷；打擾
3. **matter** [`mætər] (n.) 物質
4. **flesh** [flɛʃ] (n.) 肉；肉體

5. **pigment** [`pɪgmənt] (n.) 色素
6. **get + A + to . . .** 使 A（做到某事）
7. **owe A to B** 虧欠 B A 物品
8. **come to** 醒來；恢復神智

First, I made a piece of wood invisible. Then, I found a starving cat. I gave her some food with the drugs in it. Over several hours, the animal slowly started to become invisible. She was unconscious for quite a long time. When she finally came to [8], all I could see was the green pigment at the back of her eyes. The last time I saw her, she was just two green eyes jumping out one of my windows.

✔️ *Check Up* Fill in the blanks.

After _____ years of research, he succeeded in making creatures invisible.

Ans: nine

One Point Lesson

• But then he **shot himself** because . . .
  但之後他舉槍自盡了，因為……

----------

**shoot oneself**：舉槍自盡

28

"After successfully making the cat invisible, I knew there was the possibility of making a human invisible. I worked hard, and I had to do it quickly. I owed my landlord[1] a lot of money in rent[2]. I knew it would be perfect for me to become invisible and just disappear. I decided to mail my three books to myself to an address on the other side of London.

---

1. **landlord** [ˋlændlɔːrd] (n.) 房東
2. **rent** [rent] (n.) 房租
3. **wait for A to** 等待 A（做某事）
4. **take effect** 發揮效用
5. **extremely** [ɪkˋstriːmli] (adv.) 極度；非常
6. **desperate** [ˋdespəət] (a.) 絕望的
7. **chemical** [ˋkemɪkəl] (n.) 化學製品
8. **burn down** 燒毀

After coming back from the post office, I mixed some of the drugs for myself and drank it. While I waited for it to[3] take effect[4], there was a knock at my door. I was feeling very sick at this time and when I opened my door, my landlord looked at me, screamed and ran away. I looked at myself in the mirror and I was as white as a sheet.

I cannot describe the pain I felt over the next ten or twelve hours. By morning, I slowly became invisible. I was looking at myself in the mirror, not seeing anything of course when there was a loud bang at my door. It was the landlord. He shouted for me to open the door. I was extremely[5] desperate[6]. I didn't want them to see my chemicals[7] and equipment, so I burned the place down[8] and escaped through the window.

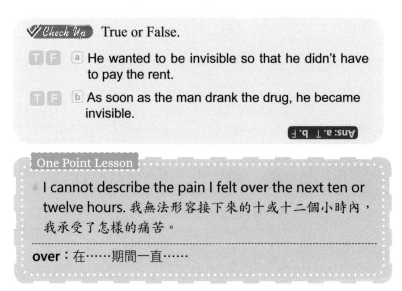

✔ *Check Up*   True or False.

T F  ⓐ He wanted to be invisible so that he didn't have to pay the rent.

T F  ⓑ As soon as the man drank the drug, he became invisible.

Ans: a. T  b. F

**One Point Lesson**

I cannot describe the pain I felt over the next ten or twelve hours. 我無法形容接下來的十或十二個小時內，我承受了怎樣的痛苦。

**over**：在⋯⋯期間一直⋯⋯

## 29

"I decided to head for the place I had sent my books. It was fun at first being invisible, but it also had plenty of[1] problems. I couldn't wear any clothes or shoes and it was extremely cold. My feet also became incredibly[2] sore[3]. Dogs and boys were a problem too. Dogs couldn't see me, but they could certainly smell me. Where there were puddles[4] of water or mud that I walked through, boys would cry out, 'Look! There are footprints[5] but nothing is making them.' A crowd of people formed[6] behind me which I had to try to escape from by finding some completely dry ground. Eventually, I was able to lose[7] my crowd of pursuers[8]."

On hearing the word "pursuers", Kemp felt a little uncomfortable[9]. He glanced[10] nervously through the window.

1. **plenty of** 很多
2. **incredibly** [ɪnˋkredɪbli] (adv.) 難以置信地
3. **sore** [sɔːr] (a.) 疼痛的
4. **puddle** [ˋpʌdl̩] (n.) 水坑；小池
5. **footprint** [ˋfʊtprɪnt] (n.) 腳印
6. **form** [fɔːrm] (v.) 形成
7. **lose** [luːz] (v.) 甩開；擺脫
8. **pursuer** [pərˋsuːər] (n.) 追捕者
9. **uncomfortable** [ʌnˋkʌmfərtəbl̩] (a.) 不自在的
10. **glance** [glæns] (v.) 瞥
11. **continue on** 繼續
12. **definitely** [ˋdefɪnətli] (adv.) 絕對地

The invisible man continued on[11] with his story. "That day, I knew I had to find shelter quickly. It was definitely[12] going to snow and I knew that if the snow fell on me, people could see me easily."

One Point Lesson

1. I had to try to escape from **by finding** some completely dry ground. 我得靠找到某些完全乾燥的地面才能逃脫。

   → **by V-ing**：藉由……達成目的。

2. **On hearing** the word "pursuers" . . .

   在一聽到「追捕者」這個字時……

   → **on V-ing**：表示「在動作發生時」。

"I found a department store[1] and waited until the doorman[2] opened the door for customers. I hurried in. I found a corner to rest in and when the store closed, I found some food to eat and some clothes to wear. I planned to sleep there, steal some money from the registers[3], and finish my disguise[4]. The problem was that I slept too well. I didn't wake up before the store opened and many people saw me.

I jumped up and ran. But I was a headless man running around the store, so I hid behind a counter[5] and tore all of my clothing off. I managed to escape just as the police arrived.

1. **department store** 百貨公司
2. **doorman** [ˋdɔːrmən] (n.) 門口接待員
3. **register** [ˋredʒɪstər] (n.) 收銀機
4. **disguise** [dɪsˋgaɪz] (n.) 偽裝
5. **counter** [ˋkaʊntər] (n.) 櫃台
6. **melt** [melt] (v.) 融化

I was very hungry, but I couldn't eat. Without any clothes on, people would be able to see the food in my stomach," the invisible man continued.

"Hmm, I never thought of that problem," commented Kemp. "What about the snow outside?"

"In the morning, all of the snow had melted[6]. But it was extremely cold outside, and I had to find something to wear as soon as I could. I could already feel myself getting sick.

✓ *Check Up* Select the wrong answer.

If he _____, people would see him.

a ate something
b wore some clothes
c slept on the street

Ans: c

"I hurried through the streets and eventually found a small costume[1] shop. It was hidden away in a small side street[2], so there were no people around. I quietly entered the shop. The owner heard me enter. As he didn't see anything, he returned to his lunch in the back. Or that was what I thought at least[3]. But the man came back again, and he had a gun in his hand. He shouted out, 'Who's there? I know someone is there. I heard you come in.' Then, he fired his gun. But it just missed me. I knew I would have to do something desperate."

"What? You killed him, didn't you?" asked Kemp.

"No! No! I didn't think so anyway. I picked up a stool[4] and hit him on the back of his head. He fell unconscious, and then I gagged[5] him and tied him up[6] with a sheet. I covered his head so that he wouldn't be able to see me putting on my disguise[7] if he came to. Kemp! I wish you wouldn't look at me like that. I had to do it. I had no choice. He had a gun! Then I took some glasses, a wig[8], some whiskers[9] and all of the money from the man's cash[10] register, and then I left."

1. **costume** [ˈkɑ:stu:m] (n.) 戲服
2. **side street** 巷道
3. **at least** 至少
4. **stool** [stu:l] (n.) 凳子
5. **gag** [gæg] (v.) 塞住……的嘴
6. **tie up** 綁起來
7. **put on disguise** 穿戴上偽裝
8. **wig** [wɪg] (n.) 假髮
9. **whisker** [ˈwɪskər] (n.) 頰鬚
10. **cash** [kæʃ] (n.) 現金

One Point Lesson

I covered his head **so that** he wouldn't be able to see me ... 我將他的頭蓋起來，這樣他才不會看到我……

**so that**：這麼一來

🎧 32

"The next thing I did was to get something to eat. I found a restaurant that had private dining rooms. I explained to the waiter that I didn't want to eat in public[1] because I was disfigured[2]."

At this point[3], the invisible man stopped talking. He seemed to turn and face[4] Kemp who was pacing[5] back and forth[6] in front of the window. The doctor didn't want Griffin to get suspicious, so he tried to keep him talking.

"Is that when you went to Iping?" the doctor asked the invisible man.

"Yes," he replied. "That is where I had all of my books sent, with my clothes and equipment. I wanted to live in a quiet village where no one would bother[7] me. I wanted to work in peace[8] and make a formula[9] to make me visible again. I want to be visible again, but only after I have done everything I want while I am invisible. I need your help for that, Kemp."

"I won't help you commit[10] crimes[11] like you have being doing up until now," replied Kemp. "You have attacked several people already."

"They will be perfectly alright. Except Thomas Marvel. When I catch up with[12] him, he will wish he had never been born. And I'll kill anyone who wants to stop me in my plans."

1. **in public** 在公眾場合
2. **disfigure** [dɪs`fɪgər] (v.) 使毀容
3. **at this point** 在這個時候
4. **face** [feɪs] (v.) 面對
5. **pace** [peɪs] 踱步
6. **back and forth** 來來回回地
7. **bother** [`bɑːðər] (v.) 打擾
8. **in peace** 安寧地；平靜地
9. **formula** [`fɔːrmjulə] (n.) 處方
10. **commit** [kə`mɪt] (v.) 犯（罪）
11. **crime** [kraɪm] (n.) 犯罪
12. **catch up with** 追上

**A** Choose the word irrelevant to the other words of the category.

**1** (a) worried     (b) concerned     (c) starving

**2** (a) transparent   (b) desperate     (c) invisible

**3** (a) extremely     (b) definitely     (c) certainly

**4** (a) agitated      (b) nervous      (c) unconscious

**B** Fill in the blanks with the given words.

> from     through     to     about     on

**1** He didn't sleep all night, thinking _____ what he should do.

**2** Did you know that later I changed _____ physics?

**3** I never had any money , so I stole it _____ my father.

**4** I mail my three books to myself to an address _____ the other side of London.

**5** I hurried _____ the streets and eventually found a small costume shop.

## C True or False.

T F ❶ Dr. Kemp found it difficult to believe the invisible man's story.

T F ❷ Dr. Kemp was not worried about sending for the police.

T F ❸ It took Griffin six years to learn how to become invisible.

T F ❹ Griffin shot his father to get all of his money.

T F ❺ It was a big problem for the invisible man to go outside.


## D Rearrange the sentences in chronological order.

❶ Griffin disguised himself with glasses, a wig, and whiskers.

❷ Griffin stole money and bought the equipment he needed.

❸ Griffin succeeded in making the cat invisible.

❹ Griffin found a department store and hurried in.

❺ Griffin burned the place down and escaped through the window.

_____ ⇨ _____ ⇨ _____ ⇨ _____ ⇨ _____

# Invisible Actually

What would you do if you were invisible for a day? H.G. Wells and other authors[1] who explored this idea all show the incredible[2] power that an invisible person would have. He or she could go anywhere secretly and steal money or valuables[3].

However, what all of these authors seemed to miss was that if a person was actually invisible, he would not be able to see! The sense of sight only works when the eyes can capture[4] light. If the back of the eye were transparent, light would pass

1. **author** [ˋɑːθər] (n.) 作者
2. **incredible** [ɪnˋkrɛdəbl̩] (a.) 不可思議的
3. **valuables** [ˋvæljubl̩z] (n.) 貴重物品

4. **capture** [ˋkæptʃər] (v.) 捕捉
5. **match** [mætʃ] (v.) 與……匹敵

right through it and no image could be sent to the brain. Now imagine an invisible person who was also blind!

Almost one hundred years after Wells's novel, the closest thing science can match[5] to an invisible man is a 'stealth[6] suit'. This suit, which is still being developed, is made of tiny pixels[7], like a computer screen that acts like clothing. The pixels would match the same color of whatever was behind the soldier. This wouldn't be true invisibility[8]. It would be more like a chameleon, which changes the color of its skin to match its background[9]. However, it is the best way to guarantee[10] invisibility without going blind!

---

6. **stealth** [stelθ] (a.)
   雷達偵察不到的；隱形的
7. **pixel** [`pɪksəl] (n.) 像素；畫素
8. **invisibility** [ˌɪnvɪzə`bɪləti] (n.) 隱形

9. **background** [`bækgraʊnd] (n.)
   背景
10. **guarantee** [ˌgærən`ti:] (v.) 保證

Traitor![1]

While Griffin was telling Kemp his plan, Kemp noticed three men coming toward his house. He walked away from the window and placed himself between it and the invisible man.

"What do you intend to[2] do here?"

1. **traitor** [ˋtreɪtər] (n.) 叛徒
2. **intend to** 打算要
3. **original** [əˋrɪdʒɪnəl] (a.) 原來的
4. **now that** 既然
5. **fully** [ˋfʊli] (adv.) 完全地

6. **rob A of B** 從 A 那裡奪走 B
7. **by this stage** 到了這一步 (stage：階段；時期)
8. **stutter** [ˋstʌtər] (v.) 結結巴巴地說
11. **let out** 發出

"My original[3] plan was to go to Spain. The weather is hot there and I could walk around with no clothes."

"That would be a good idea. When will you leave?" asked Kemp.

"I won't. Not now that[4] I've suddenly met you. You are a scientist, and there is no one better than you to fully[5] understand the wonderful discovery I have made. You can help me better than that tramp who robbed me of[6] everything."

Kemp was extremely worried by this stage[7].

"Had. . . hadn't y-y-you b-b-better get your b-b-books from him first?" stuttered[8] Kemp. "I read in the newspapers that he asked the police to lock him up in prison."

"I will get to him. Trust me, I will," promised the invisible man. He let out[9] a laugh that made him seem completely crazy.

One Point Lesson

He placed himself **between** it **and** the invisible man.
他將自己站在它和隱形人之間。

**between A and B**：在 A 和 B 之間

## 34

It was fortunate[1] because his laughter covered the sound of people entering the house through the front door.

"We can do anything, Kemp. We can steal! We can kill! We can punish[2] anyone who will try to stop us," said a crazed[3] Griffin.

"But you are invisible. I am not," said Kemp. "Why are you asking me to put myself into[4] this dangerous position[5]? I've already given you . . ."

"Shhh! What was that noise?" said Griffin.

"I didn't hear any noise."

Kemp was determined to[6] not let Griffin know some men had entered his house. "There is no way I'm going to help you in your plan. I think you should publish[7] your work for the rest of the world. I will help you work on a formula to make

1. **fortunate** [ˈfɔːrtʃənət] (a.) 幸運的
2. **punish** [ˈpʌnɪʃ] (v.) 懲罰
3. **crazed** [kreɪzd] (a.) 狂熱的
4. **put A into** 將 A 置於（某情況之下）
5. **position** [pəˈzɪʃən] (n.) 處境；立場
6. **be determined to** 下定決心要（做某事）
7. **publish** [ˈpʌblɪʃ] (v.) 發表；公開
8. **cut off** 打斷（談話）
9. **footstep** [ˈfʊtstɛp] (n.) 腳步聲

you visible again though. Perhaps we can ask another scientist to help."

Griffin cut him off[8] again. "Footsteps[9]! They are coming upstairs. You better not have told anyone that I am here. If you have . . ." Griffin warned.

"I haven't told anyone."

Griffin started to walk toward the door, but Kemp got in his way.

"Traitor! You have betrayed me." screamed the invisible man.

✔️ *Check Up* Fill in the blanks.

Griffin's _____ kept him from noticing some men entering the house.

Ans: laughter

One Point Lesson

• **You better** not have told anyone that I am here.
你最好沒有告訴任何人我在這裡。

--------

**You better** = You had better：你最好……

## 35

The invisible man then started to take off the dressing gown. Kemp reached for the door and opened it violently. Griffin tried to follow him, but Kemp pushed him back into the room. He wanted to lock the invisible man in the room, but when the door slammed, it made the key fall out.

Kemp held onto[1] the door very hard, but Griffin managed to yank[2] it open a little. Griffin wedged[3] his body between the door and the door frame[4]. He put out his invisible hand and wrapped his fingers around Kemp's throat. Kemp let go of[5] the door handle, and a flying dressing gown came out into the hall. In a flash[6], the dressing gown had Kemp pinned[7] to the floor at the top of the stairs.

Halfway[8] up the stairs, an astonished Chief of Police, Colonel Adye, watched as Kemp fought with a dressing gown that was moving wildly all

1. **hold onto** 抓住
2. **yank** [jæŋk] (v.) 猛拉
3. **wedge** [wedʒ] (v.) 擠入
4. **frame** [freɪm] (n.) 邊框
5. **let go of** 放開……
6. **in a flash** 一瞬間；馬上
7. **pin** [pɪn] (v.) 壓住；使彈不得
8. **halfway** [ˋhæfˋweɪ] (adv.) 中途地

9. **directly** [dɪˋrekli] (adv.) 直接地
10. **fingernail** [ˋfɪŋgərneɪl] (n.) 手指甲
11. **dig (in/into)** 刺；插入
12. **sharp** [ʃɑːrp] (a.) 劇烈的
13. **belly** [ˋbeli] (n.) 腹部
14. **drive** [draɪv] (v.) 用力打入

by itself. The next moment, the Colonel saw a
dressing gown directly[9] in front of him.
Suddenly, he felt sharp fingernails[10] digging[11]
into his throat and then a sharp[12] pain in his
belly[13] as the invisible man drove[14] his knee into
the man's stomach. Next thing he knew, he was
lying at the bottom of the stairs.

"We lost him." cried Kemp. His face was
covered with blood.

**One Point Lesson**

When the door slammed, it **made** the key **fall** out.
當門用力關上時，鑰匙掉了出來。

--------------------------------------------------

**make + A + 原形動詞**：使 A 做某動作

## 36

It took quite a few minutes for the men to settle[1] their nerves[2]. Kemp took the Colonel to his office and they had a drink together.

"That man is insane[3]. He has lost all of his sense[4] of reasoning[5]. He will kill a lot of people if we don't stop him," said Kemp.

"We must catch him, and we will," replied the Colonel.

1. **settle** [ˋsetḷ] (v.) 使安定
2. **nerves** [nɜːvz] (n.) 緊張；憂慮
3. **insane** [ɪnˋseɪn] (a.) 瘋狂的
4. **sense** [sens] (n.) 觀念；意識
5. **reasoning** [ˋriːzənɪŋ] (n.) 講理
6. **area** [ˋerɪə] (n.) 區域

"We have to do it while he is in this area[6]. He wants to get his books from Marvel. That is the only thing that will keep him here. Every building must be kept locked. We must stop him from[7] sleeping, eating or getting clothes."

The colonel agreed with Kemp. "Yes. You must come with me to help organize[8] the search[9]. You know the most about him."

"Alright," agreed Kemp. "We should use dogs too. They can't see him, but they can smell him. Also, tell your men to keep their weapons[10] hidden. He'll try to use any weapon he finds."

The colonel listened carefully to Kemp. "Good. Anything else?"

"Yes, put broken glass all over the roads. It will cut his feet."

7. **stop A from V-ing**
   阻止 A 做某事
8. **organize** [ˈɔːrɡənaɪz] (v.) 組織

9. **search** [sɜːrtʃ] (n.) 搜索
10. **weapon** [ˈwepən] (n.) 武器

One Point Lesson

Also, tell your men to **keep** their weapons **hidden**.
還有，叫你的手下要將武器藏好。

**keep + A + 形容詞**：使 A 保持某狀態

🎧 37

The two men left and went to organize the manhunt[1]. By early afternoon, the whole country knew of the dangerous invisible man. Warnings[2] were put everywhere, schools were closed and all buildings and houses were kept locked. All around Port Burdock, men armed[3] themselves with guns, knives and clubs[4]. Dogs were sent out, trying to find the invisible man's scent[5].

1. **manhunt** [ˋmænhʌnt] (n.) 搜捕
2. **warning** [ˋwɔːrnɪŋ] (n.) 警告
3. **arm** [ɑːrm] (v.) 使武裝
4. **club** [klʌb] (n.) 棍棒
5. **scent** [sent] (n.) 氣味
6. **report** [rɪˋpɔːrt] (n.) 謠傳

Over the next few days, there were many reports[6] of the invisible man. In Hintondean which was seven or eight miles from Port Burdock, several men claimed[7] that they heard a strange voice crying, laughing, and moaning as it passed through a field.

When Colonel Adye heard this, he said to Kemp, "He must be staying out of the towns. He knows that by now, we have everything locked and guarded[8]."

"Yes, but he's desperate. Hopefully[9] he will do something stupid that will lead us to him," said Kemp.

However, the invisible man was able to avoid being captured. In fact, unknown[10] to everyone, the invisible man continued to feel stronger and more determined to remain[11] free.

---

7. **claim** [kleɪm] (v.) 聲稱
8. **guard** [gɑːrd] (v.) 看守
9. **hopefully** [ˋhoupfəli] (adv.) 但願；懷希望地

10. **unknown** [ʌnˋnoʊn] (a.) 不知道的
11. **remain + adj.** 維持（某狀態）

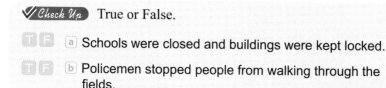

Check Up　True or False.

T F　a Schools were closed and buildings were kept locked.

T F　b Policemen stopped people from walking through the fields.

Ans: a. T b. F

Later that day, Dr. Kemp was having lunch when his housekeeper brought him a letter. It had come from Hintondean. He quickly opened the letter and read:

*To all the residents[1] in Port Burdock:*

*You are all very smart. You have made it very difficult for me to survive[2] in the Port Burdock area. You have proven[3] that you are all against[4] me. You will pay for[5] this. I will start a reign[6] of terror. Tell your Colonel Adye that Port Burdock's new ruler[7] is The Invisible Man. This reign of terror will begin with the execution[8] of Dr. Kemp. He may hide or protect[9] himself with all the guards in the world, but I will kill him. If any of you help Kemp, I will know, and you will be the next to die.*

1. **resident** [ˋrɛzɪdənt] (n.) 居民
2. **survive** [səˋvaɪv] (v.) 生存
3. **prove** [pruːv] (v.) 證明
4. **against** [əˋgɛnst] (prep.) 反對
5. **pay for** 為……付出代價
6. **reign** [rɪn] (n.) 統治

Kemp called his housekeeper. "Please make sure[10] all of the windows and doors are locked at all times," he instructed[11] her. He went upstairs and got his gun. He was very angry and shouted out, "We will catch him even if[12] I am the bait[13]!"

He quickly wrote a note, gave it to his housekeeper and told her to take it to the police station. "Stay at the police station. Do not come back to this house until I tell you to." he told her.

---

7. **ruler** [ˋruːlər] (n.) 統治者

8. **execution** [ˌeksɪˋkjuːʃən] (n.) 處決

9. **protect** [prəˋtekt] (v.) 保護

10. **make sure** 確認

11. **instruct** [ɪnˋstrʌkt] (v.) 指示

12. **even if** 即使

13. **bait** [beɪt] (n.) 餌

101

The housekeeper left, but less than[1] an hour later, Colonel Adye was at his house.

"It's your housekeeper," he said. "She said she was delivering[2] a note to me from you. On her way to the station, it was snatched[3] out of her hand."

"Oh no!" exclaimed Kemp. "I had a plan to try to catch him, but now he knows the plan."

Their conversation was cut off by the sound of breaking glass.

"He's here now! He's trying to get in through the bedroom windows!" Kemp cried.

"Alright. Give me your gun. I'll go and get the tracking[4] dogs," said Adye.

Kemp gave him his gun and slammed the door bolt shut as soon as he left. Adye walked out of the house, but behind him, he heard a voice, "Stop!"

Just at that moment, Adye felt a sharp pain in his back, and he was then flat[5] on the ground. He felt the gun being ripped[6] out of his hand. He looked above him and saw the gun floating[7] in midair[8].

1. **less than** 不到
2. **deliver** [dɪˋlɪvər] (v.) 傳送
3. **snatch** [snætʃ] (v.) 搶奪
4. **track** [træk] (v.) 追蹤
5. **flat** [flæt] (a.) 平躺的
6. **rip** [rɪp] (v.) 扯掉
7. **float** [floʊt] (v.) 飄浮
8. **midair** [mɪdˋɛr] (n.) 半空

"I would kill you if I didn't have better things to do," said the voice. "Get up!"

Adye slowly stood up.

"Now go back into the house."

"Kemp won't let me back in." Adye said.

✓ **Check Up** Choose the correct answer.

What did Dr. Kemp do?

ⓐ He slammed the door bolt shut.

ⓑ He broke the window glass.

ⓒ He snatched the note from the housekeeper.

Ans: a

**One Point Lesson**

• Kemp . . . slammed the door bolt shut **as soon as** he left.
凱普⋯⋯等他一離開，就馬上將門用力閂上。

---

**as soon as**：一⋯⋯就⋯⋯

🎧40

Kemp stood watching all of this by the window of the kitchen. He thought, "Adye should fire his gun." But then he saw the gun floating in the air and realized what had happened. He saw Adye walking toward the house. Suddenly, Adye jumped back and tried to grab the gun. There was a shot, and Adye fell to the ground. Kemp was shocked.

He couldn't move or think, but the sound of smashing wood made him move from his place in the kitchen. He looked through the front window and saw two policemen coming to his house. They rang the doorbell, and Kemp let them in.

"He has a gun and an ax," Kemp warned them. "He'll be inside at any moment[1]."

Just as he was giving the policemen a poker each, a gun and ax appeared in the room.

One policeman managed to stop a blow[2] from the ax. The other policeman knocked the gun out of[3] the invisible man's hand. Next, one policeman hit something soft[4], and there was a moan[5] of pain. The ax fell to the floor. The policeman struck[6] his poker in the same place, but it only came down hard on the floor.

"Where did he go?" asked one policeman. "I don't know. I hit him but he must have escaped. Dr. Kemp is gone too," said the other policeman.

1. **at any moment** 隨時
2. **blow** [bloʊ] (n.) 猛擊
3. **knock** *A* **out of**
   將 A 從……打下來
4. **soft** [sɑːft] (a.) 柔軟的
5. **moan** [moʊn] (n.) 呻吟
6. **strike** [straɪk] (v.) 打
   (strike-struck-struck/stricken)

During the fighting[1], Dr. Kemp had jumped out a window and headed for his closest[2] neighbor. He banged[3] on the door, but as people were so afraid of the invisible man, no one opened the door to him. He decided to find somewhere else to hide. He deliberately[4] walked over a road that had broken glass all over it.

Kemp ran toward Port Burdock, but he could

1. **fighting** [`faɪtɪŋ] (n.) 打鬥
2. **close** [klouz] (a.) 靠近的
3. **bang** [bæŋ] (v.) 猛擊
4. **deliberately** [dɪ`lɪbərətli] (adv.) 故意地
5. **pick up** 拾起

*The Invisible Man*

hear the sound of footsteps behind him.

"The invisible man! He's behind me," he cried. Women and children screamed and ran. Men in the town picked up[5] shovels[6].

Kemp yelled out, "Form[7] a line." Just at that moment, he was hit from behind. He then felt a fist smash into his jaw[8]. Griffin then grabbed Kemp's throat and put a knee into his chest.

6. **shovel** [ˈʃʌvəl] (n.) 鏟子
7. **form** [fɔːrm] (v.) 排成特定隊形

8. **jaw** [dʒɑː] (n.) 下巴

That was the end of the invisible man; but his story is not quite[1] finished. There is a wealthy[2] man who lives in Port Stowe. He used to be a tramp, but now he is the owner of an inn.

For those visiting the inn, he willingly[3] tells the story of the invisible man. He tells his guests how he outsmarted[4] the police who wanted to take the money in his pockets away from him. He also claims that he never saw the three notebooks that Jack Griffin wrote. He said that Griffin hid the books somewhere else. But in his

---

1. **quite** [kwaɪt] (adv.) 完全地
2. **wealthy** [ˋwelθi] (a.) 富有的
3. **willingly** [ˋwɪlɪŋli] (adv.) 樂意地
4. **outsmart** [ˋaʊtˋsmɑːrt] (v.) 以機智打敗

5. **examine** [ɪgˋzæmɪn] (v.) 檢查
6. **once** [wʌns] (conj.) 一旦
7. **recover** [rɪˋkʌvər] (v.) 康復
8. **on many occasions** 在許多機會下

free time, Mr. Thomas Marvel sits in his study and examines[5] the strange code.

"Once[6] I find out what all of this means, I'll be able to, well, I'll never do what he did."

Kemp and Colonel Adye, who recovered[7] from his gunshot, questioned Marvel about the books on many occasions[8]. But no one will know what happened to the books until Marvel leaves this world.

✅ *Check Up* Answer the question.

What happened to the tramp, Thomas Marvel?

_____.

**Ans: He became rich with the stolen money and bought an inn.**

### One Point Lesson

He **used to be** a tramp, but now he is the owner of an inn.
他以前曾經是流浪漢，但現在他是一間旅館的所有人。

**used to + be + N**：以前曾經是……

**A** Match the two parts of each sentence.

1 snatch •        • a An instrument used for digging

2 shovel •        • b To take or grasp quickly

3 yank •          • c A strong, sudden pull

4 formula •       • d One who betrays another's trust

5 traitor •       • e A method to make a chemical
                      composition

**B** Read the sentences and write down who said
each sentence.

the invisible man    Colonel Adye    Dr. Kemp    the policeman

1 She said she was delivering a note to me from you. _____

2 We can punish anyone who will try to stop us.    _____

3 We must catch him, and we will.                  _____

4 We will catch him even if I am the bait!          _____

5 I hit him but he must have escaped.              _____

## C Choose the correct answer.

**1** Who had the three books that belonged to the invisible man?

(a) Dr. Kemp    (b) Colonel Adye    (c) Thomas Marvel

**2** When the invisible man heard footsteps, what did he do first?

(a) He ran to get his gun.

(b) He tore off his clothes.

(c) He knocked Dr. Kemp to the floor.

**3** What happened to the invisible man when he died?

(a) His veins and bones started to appear.

(b) His body could not be felt.

(c) His body became as hard as stone.

## D Rearrange the sentence in chronological order.

**1** The invisible man broke into Kemp's house with an ax.

**2** The invisible man sent a letter to Dr. Kemp.

**3** The tramp, Marvel, became the rich owner of an inn.

**4** A policeman hit the invisible man with a poker.

**5** The invisible man's body became visible.

**6** Dr. Kemp escaped from his house during the fight.

_____ ⇨ _____ ⇨ _____ ⇨ _____ ⇨ _____ ⇨ _____

# Appendixes

# 1 Basic Grammar

要增強英文閱讀理解能力，應練習找出英文的主結構。
要擁有良好的英語閱讀能力，首先要理解英文的段落結構。

### 「英文的主要句型結構比較簡單」

所有的英文文章都是由主詞和動詞所構成的，無論文章再怎麼長或複雜，它的架構一定是「主詞和動詞」，而「補語」和「受詞」是做補充主詞和動詞的角色。

He knew / that she told a lie / at the party.

他知道　　　　她說了謊　　　　在舞會上
⇨ 他知道她在舞會上說謊的事。

As she was walking / in the garden, / she smelled /

當她行走　　　　　　在花園　　　　她聞到味道

something wet.

某樣濕濕的東西。
⇨ 她走在花園時聞到潮溼的味道。

He knew / that she told a lie / at the party.
他知道　/ 她說了一個謊　/ 在那個派對上。

一篇文章要分成幾個有意義的詞組？

可放入（／）符號來區隔有意義詞組的地方，一般是在（1）「主詞＋動詞」之後；（2）and 和 but 等連接詞之前；（3）that、who 等關係代名詞之前；（4）副詞子句的前後，會用（／）符號來區隔。初學者可能在一篇文章中畫很多（／）符號，但隨著閱讀實力的提升，（／）會減少。時間一久，在不太複雜的文章中，即使不畫（／）符號，也能一眼就理解整句的意義。

使用（／）符號來閱讀理解英語篇章
1. 能熟悉英文的句型和構造。
2. 可加速閱讀速度。

該方法對於需要邊聽邊理解的英文聽力也有很好的效果。
從現在開始，早日丟棄過去理解文章的習慣吧！

## 以直接閱讀理解的方式，重新閱讀《隱形人》

　　從原文中摘錄一小段。以具有意義的詞組將文章做斷句區分，重新閱讀並做理解練習。

As she was walking / in the garden, / she smelled / something wet.
當她走　　　　　　／ 在花園裡，　　／ 她聞到　　／ 某個濕濕的東西。

In the darkness of a February night, / a stranger dressed in a wide-brimmed hat and very long coat / got off a train / at Bramblehurst.
在二月的一個黑夜裡，　　　　　　　　／ 一個穿戴著闊邊帽和長大衣的陌
生人　　　　　　　　　　　　　／ 離開了一班火車 / 在布蘭堡赫斯特。

It was bitterly cold, / but there were no carriages.
天氣非常酷寒，　　　／ 但是卻沒有馬車。

The man had to carry his suitcase / for several hours / through a snowstorm / to reach the small town of Iping.
這名男子得帶著他的行李　　　　　／好幾個小時　　　／穿越暴風雪　　　／到伊坪這個小鎮。

When he arrived, / he went to the Coach and Horses Inn.
當他抵達時，　　　／他前往「馬車與馬」旅館。

The people in the inn saw / a dark figure stumble in.
旅館裡的人看到　　　　　　／一個黑色身影跌跌撞撞地走進來。

"I want a room and a fire. / Quickly please!" / the stranger demanded.
「我要一間房間，還要生火。/ 請快一點！」/ 陌生人要求道。

The owner of the inn said, / "I'm Mrs. Hall. / Please come this way."
旅館的主人說，　　　　　／「我是霍爾太太。/ 請往這邊走。」

The woman showed the stranger to his room.
這個女人帶陌生人去他的房間。

She left / and soon returned with some food.
她離開了 / 然後很快帶了些食物回來。

The room was very warm now, / but the man was still wearing / his hat, coat and gloves.
房間裡現在已經很溫暖了，　　／但這名男子仍然穿戴著　　／他的帽子、外套和手套。

"I can take your coat for you," / Mrs. Hall said.
「我可以幫你拿外套。」　　　／霍爾太太說。

"No!" / snapped the stranger.
「不！」/ 陌生人厲聲喊。

"Alright," said the woman / as she left the room.
「好吧。」這女人說 ／當她離開房間。

In the kitchen, / Mrs. Hall realized / she had forgotten the mustard, / so she took it up to the man.
在廚房裡， ／霍爾太太發現 ／她忘了拿芥末，
／於是她將芥末拿上去給這名男子。

She knocked on the door / and opened it.
她敲敲門 ／然後將它打開。

She stood in the doorway, / stunned.
她站在門口， ／目瞪口呆。

The strange man had large bulky bandages / around his head.
這名陌生男子包著笨重的大繃帶 ／環繞在頭部。

All she could see / were his blue glasses, a shiny pink nose and some hair / poking through the bandages.
她所能看到的 ／是他的藍色眼鏡，一個發亮的粉紅色鼻子和一些頭髮
／從繃帶之間露出來。

"I . . . I will take your things now, / sir," / she stammered.
「我⋯⋯我現在幫你拿東西， ／先生。」／她結結巴巴地說。

"Leave the hat," / he demanded.
「留著帽子。」／他要求道。

Mrs. Hall noticed / that the stranger was still wearing his gloves / and he was holding a napkin over his face.
霍爾太太注意到 ／這名陌生人仍然戴著手套
／而且他還拿餐巾遮住臉。

He was wearing a dark dressing gown / of which he had the collar turned up high.
他穿著一件深色的浴袍 ／他還把領子往上拉高。

# Guide to Listening Comprehension

When listening to the story, use some of the techniques shown below. If you take time to study some phonetic characteristics of English, listening will be easier.

### Get in the flow of English.

English creates a rhythm formed by combinations of strong and weak stress intonations. Each word has its particular stress that combines with other words to form the overall pattern of stress or rhythm in a particular sentence.

When speaking and listening to English, it is essential to get in the flow of the rhythm of English. It takes a lot of practice to get used to such a rhythm. So, you need to start by identifying the stressed syllable in a word.

*Listen for the strongly stressed words and phrases.*

In English, key words and phrases that are essential to the meaning of a sentence are stressed louder. Therefore, pay attention to the words stressed with a higher pitch. When listening to an English recording for the first time, what matters most is to listen for a general understanding of what you hear. Do not try to hear every single word. Most of the unstressed words are articles or auxiliary verbs, which don't play an important role in the general context. At this level, you can ignore them.


*Pay attention to liaisons.*

In reading English, words are written with a space between them. There isn't such an obvious guide when it comes to listening to English. In oral English, there are many cases when the sounds of words are linked with adjacent words.

For instance, let's think about the phrase "take off," which can be used in "take off your clothes." "Take off your clothes" doesn't sound like [teɪk ɔːf] with each of the words completely and clearly separated from the others. Instead, it sounds as if almost all the words in context are slurred together, [ˈteɪkɔːf], for a more natural sound.

## Shadow the voice of the native speaker.

Finally, you need to mimic the voice of the native speaker. Once you are sure you know how to pronounce all the words in a sentence, try to repeat them like an echo. Listen to the book again, but this time you should try a fun exercise while listening to the English.

This exercise is called "shadowing." The word "shadow" means a dark shade that is formed on a surface. When used as a verb, the word refers to the action of following someone or something like a shadow. In this exercise, pretend you are a parrot and try to shadow the voice of the native speaker.

Try to mimic the reader's voice by speaking at the same speed, with the same strong and weak stresses on words, and pausing or stopping at the same points.

Experts have already proven this technique to be effective. If you practice this shadowing exercise, your English speaking and listening skills will improve by leaps and bounds. While shadowing the native speaker, don't forget to pay attention to the meaning of each phrase and sentence.

Listen to what you want to shadow many times. Start out by just trying to shadow a few words or a sentence.

 Mimic the CD out loud. You can shadow everything the speaker says as if you are singing a round, or you also can speak simultaneously with the recorded voice of the native speaker.

 As you practice more, try to shadow more. For instance, shadow a whole sentence or paragraph instead of just a few words.

# Listening Guide

**Chapter One** pages 14–15

In the darkness of a February night, a stranger ( ❶ ) ( ) a wide-brimmed hat and very long coat got off a train at Bramblehurst. It was ( ❷ ) cold, but there were no carriages. The man ( ❸ ) ( ) carry his suitcase for several hours through a snow-storm to reach the small town of Iping. When he arrived, he went to the Coach and Horses Inn. The people in the inn saw a dark figure ( ❹ ) ( ).

"I want a room and a fire. Quickly, please!" the stranger demanded.

The owner of the inn said, "I'm Mrs. Hall. Please come this way."

The ( ❺ ) showed the stranger to his room.

She left and soon returned with some food. The room was very warm now, but the man was still wearing his hat, coat and gloves.

"I can take your coat for you," Mrs. Hall said.

"No!" snapped the stranger.

"Alright," said the woman as she left the room.

以下為《隱形人》各章節的前半部。一開始若能聽清楚發音，之後就沒有聽力的負擔。先聽過摘錄的章節，之後再反覆聆聽括弧內單字的發音，並仔細閱讀各種發音的說明。以下都是以英語的典型發音為基礎，所做的簡易說明，即使這裡未提到的發音，也可以配合音檔反覆聆聽，如此一來聽力必能更上層樓。

**❶ dressed in**：當這兩個單字連續唸時，dressed 結尾的無聲子音 [t]，會和 in 開頭的母音 [ɪ] 結合，變化成 [tɪn] 的發音。

**❷ bitterly**：在發音上, 當 -tt- 接 r 的時候，t 和 r 的發音結合。另外，像 it is 連唸時，t 會和 is 開頭的母音 [ɪ] 結合。

**❸ had to**：這裡 had 的尾音 [d] 後面接無聲子音 [t] 時，[d] 的發音會直接省略，變成 [hæ tu] 的發音。

**❹ stumble in**：當無聲字音 [s] 和 [t] 連唸時，會變化成有聲子音 [d]，成為 [sd] 的發音。另外，像 stranger 一字中，子音 [s] 後接 [tr]，則會變化成 [sdr] 的發音。

**❺ woman**：woman 一字的發音較為特別，單數時，o 發 [ʊ] 的音，然而在複數（women）時，o 卻發 [ɪ] 的音，要特別注意。

In the kitchen, Mrs. Hall realized she had forgotten the mustard, so she ( **❶** ) (     ) (     ) to the man. She knocked on the door and opened it. She stood in the doorway, stunned. The strange man had large bulky bandages around his head. All she ( **❷** ) see were his blue glasses, a shiny pink nose and some hair poking through the bandages.

"I . . . I will take your things now, sir," she stammered.

"Leave the hat," he ( **❸** ).

Mrs. Hall ( **❹** ) (     ) the stranger was still wearing his gloves and he was holding a napkin over his face. He was wearing a dark dressing gown of which he had the collar turned up high. Around his neck, he had tied a scarf. Every part of his body was ( **❺** ) covered.

"Y-y-yes, sir," said the shocked Mrs. Hall.

"He must have had a terrible accident," Mrs. Hall thought.

Some time later, she returned for the tray. After eating and becoming warm, the stranger's ( **❻** ) had much improved and he now said, "I left some baggage at Bramblehurst Station, Mrs. Hall. Is there some way to bring it here?"

**❶ took it up:** 這三個單字的尾音剛好都是無聲子音，所接的字的開頭是母音，在這種情況下，前一個字的子音會和後一個字開頭的母音結合，實際唸起來的發音為 [tʊ kɪ tʌp]。

**❷ could:** could、would 和 should 三字的 -ould 都是 [ʊd] 的發音。

**❸ demanded:** demand 這個字有兩個音節，由於重音在第二個音節，加上過去式後，過去式 ed 的 e 發音為較輕音的 [ə]。

**❹ noticed that:** noticed 的尾音為無聲子音 [t]，後接 that 時，兩者結合發音為 [ð]。

**❺ completely:** 當遇到音標有 [tl] 或 [tn] 連在一起的發音時，[t] 在讀音上會變成接近「嗯」的喉音。

**❻ mood:** mood 的發音為 [mud]，oo 發長音 [u]。同樣的情形會出現在以 p、t、k、s、b、d、g 等子音為首的單字中。

# 4

# Listening Comprehension

🎧 46 **A** Listen to the MP3 and fill in the blanks.

① The man was wearing a dark dressing gown of which he had the collar _____.

② Suddenly Mr. Hall felt himself _____ out of the room.

③ _____ been a dark room was now lit by a candle.

④ The two men realized they _____ feel the invisible man.

⑤ By early afternoon, the _____ the dangerous invisible man.

⑥ He deliberately _____ had broken glass all over it.

⑦ A shovel _____ and slammed into something soft.

🎧 47 **B** Listen to the MP3. True or False.

T F ① _____

T F ② _____

T F ③ _____

T F ④ _____

T F ⑤ _____

*The Invisible Man*

🎧 48 Ⓒ Listen to the MP3 and choose the correct answer.

**1** _____?

    (a) Because she was curious about the stranger.

    (b) Because she thought that he would be able to help her.

    (c) Because there weren't many other guests at that time.

**2** _____?

    (a) Women hitting him.

    (b) Boys seeing his footprints.

    (c) Glass lying on the road.

🎧 49 Ⓓ Listen to the MP3 and write down the sentences. Rearrange the sentences in chronological order.

**1** _____

**2** _____

**3** _____

**4** _____

**5** _____

_____ ⇨ _____ ⇨ _____ ⇨ _____ ⇨ _____

# Translation

## 作者簡介　p. 4

### 赫伯特・喬治・維爾斯
（Herbert George Wells, 1866–1946）

　　1866 年生於英國布羅姆利，父親是個失敗的工匠，母親則當過女傭。13 歲時他離開學校，成為布店的學徒。家人們認為這會是個適合他的工作，但他並不喜歡，這段在布店的不快經歷也成為日後創作小說《基普斯》（*Kipps*）的靈感。維爾斯年幼時會閱讀任何手邊找得到的讀物，讓思緒漫遊在遙遠虛構的時空裡。

　　1883 年，他在米德赫斯特文法學校得到助教職位。1884 年，他贏得獎學金進入英國皇家科學院。當時最好的生物學家湯瑪斯・亨利・赫胥黎是他的生物老師，並對他的人生起了極其強烈的影響。大學時代，維爾斯創立並編輯《科學學校期刊》。

　　1888 年畢業後，維爾斯在接下來幾年從事教學與寫作。1891 年，他在科學上的重要論文《單一性的再發現》（*The Rediscovery of the Unique*）出版。1895 年，維爾斯以《時間機器》（*Time Machine*）奠定其科幻小說家的地位。故事講述一個沈迷於時空旅行的夢想家，替自己建造一座時間機器，並穿越八百萬年到達未來世界。由於小說大獲成功，自那開始維爾斯便不用再教書或為錢財煩惱。

　　《時間機器》出版不久後，維爾斯又創作其他成功的小說，如《莫洛博士島》（*The Island of Doctor Moreau*, 1896）、《隱形人》（*The Invisible Man*, 1897）與《世界大戰》（*The War of the Worlds*, 1898），維爾斯建立了現代科幻小說的原型，更因此被視為現代科幻小說之父，有時也被叫做時空機器旅人。維爾斯也有關於政治、科技、未來的非虛構著作，以支持他對人性與社會的論點，以及對世界走向的看法。

赫伯特‧喬治‧維爾斯於 1946 年去世，享壽 80 歲，當時手頭上的計畫是討論核戰的危險。維爾斯作為科幻小說的先驅，過去夢想著人類文明的更進化，至今仍值得世人的尊敬與欽佩。

## 故事簡介 　p.5

《隱形人》的故事開頭是個寒冷的暴風雪冬日，有位陌生人來到了英國鄉間的小旅館。在那時，冬天旅行並不尋常，但更可疑的是，陌生人的臉被繃帶纏繞著。整個村莊都因這陌生人的到來而騷動，接著開始發生前所未聞的事件，像是身分不明的搶匪闖入教士的住處等。

終於，在旅館房東與房東太太試圖追趕下，陌生人解開他的繃帶。他在眾人面前展露他隱形人的身分，之後便立即消失了。經過長途漫步，隱形人進入凱普博士的住所。凱普博士不想忍受隱形人莽撞的行為。然而不幸地，隱形人已喪失清晰思考的能力。

1897 年 H‧G‧維爾斯出版此書，成為他科幻小說的經典著作。內容講述一個男人發明可將人隱形的藥劑，但這位隱形人卻做了許多錯事。H‧G‧維爾斯描繪一個精妙的科學性發現，也描述出一個格格不入的人，處於絕望深淵的孤獨生活，其筆法值得讀者認知賞識。

## The Invisible Man 隱形人

我是個既冷酷又急躁的人，任何人想阻礙我，我都會殺了他。很不幸的，隱形並不如我想像中那麼輕鬆，我需要錢和衣服來維持溫飽；然而，每次我試圖要得到這兩樣東西時，卻總是給自己帶來許多麻煩。我試著要其他人幫助我，但是他們害怕我的能力。我不能相信任何人。

## Dr. Kemp 凱普博士

我是個老實的科學研究家，居住在一座海邊的小鎮上。有一天，一位大學的老同學意外來訪；而你看，這位老朋友竟然就是隱形人！我必須決定到底要幫助他，還是將他交給警察。他似乎相當危險，能夠為了得到想要的東西，而殺害無辜的人。

## Marvel 馬佛

我是個住在鄉下的窮乞丐，人們忽視我的存在，我到哪裡都找不到工作。我想，這就是隱形人選上我幫助他的原因吧！但是，我並不想幫助他，他真的嚇壞我了！在幫他搶劫銀行之後，我帶著那筆錢和他的研究書籍逃跑了。我好怕他會找到我並且把我殺了！

## Mr. Hall and Mrs. Hall 霍爾夫婦

　　我們在伊坪這座鄉間小鎮裡，經營一間寧靜的小旅館。我們想要過平靜的生活，但這一切卻在那個陌生人來臨的夜晚破滅了。在他待在我們這裡的幾個星期中，我們經常可以聽到他在發脾氣，還砸壞瓶子和家具。他總是從頭到腳都用衣物蓋住，即使在溫暖的房間裡也不例外。這個人真的很奇怪。

## [ 第一章 ] 神祕的陌生人

`p. 14–15` 二月裡的某個夜晚，黑暗中，一名頭戴闊邊帽、穿著超長大衣的陌生人，在布蘭堡赫斯特的火車站下車。天氣十分酷寒，卻沒有馬車可以搭。這人得帶著他的手提箱穿越暴風雪，走好幾個小時到伊坪這座小鎮。當他抵達時，他前往「馬車與馬」旅館。旅館裡的人看到一個黑色的身影跌跌撞撞地走進來。

　　「我要一間房間，還要生火，請快一點！」陌生人要求道。

　　旅館的主人說：「我是霍爾太太，這邊請。」

　　這位婦人帶著陌生人到他的房間。

　　她離開後，很快帶了一些食物回來。房間現在已經很溫暖了，但這名男子仍然穿戴著他的帽子、大衣和手套。

　　「我可以幫你拿外套。」霍爾太太說。

　　「不要！」陌生人厲聲喊。

　　「好的。」婦人說著離開房間。

`p. 16–17` 回到廚房後，霍爾太太發現她忘了拿芥末給他，便拿著芥末要去給這名男子。她敲敲門，把門打開，卻在門口看得目瞪口呆：她看到陌生人的頭包著笨重的大繃帶，只見得到他藍色的眼鏡，發亮的粉紅色鼻子，還有些從繃帶之間露出來的頭髮。

「我……我現在幫你拿東西，先生。」她結結巴巴地説。

「把帽子留著。」他要求道。

霍爾太太注意到，這名陌生人仍然戴著手套，而且他還拿餐巾遮住臉。他穿著一件深色的浴袍，還把領子往上拉高，他的脖子上也繫了一條圍巾，全身上下都裹著。

「是……是……是的，先生。」震驚的霍爾太太説。

「他一定遭遇過可怕的意外。」她心想。

一段時間後，她回去拿食物的托盤。在吃過東西、取過暖之後，陌生人的心情好了許多，他現在説：「霍爾太太，我在布蘭堡赫斯特車站留了一些行李，有什麼辦法可以把它們拿過來？」

p. 18–19 「今天晚上路況不好，明天早上我先生會幫你帶過來。在這樣的風雪中，是很容易發生意外的。」她回答。

「是啊，意外。我也發生過意外。」

「是什麼樣的意……」霍爾太太開口問。

「別管那麼多，」陌生人説。「妳只要知道我是個科學家，還有我所有的設備都在我的行李裡就夠了。我需要儘快拿到行李，我在做一個非常重要的實驗。」

霍爾太太離開時心想：「他真是個神祕的人。」

她很快回到酒吧，告訴她的顧客關於這名神祕男子的事。其中一名顧客，泰迪・亨佛瑞説：「哈！我敢打賭，他一定是在躲警察。他才沒發生過什麼意外！」

「誰在躲警察？」他們後面有個聲音説道——那是霍爾先生。

「今晚剛有個陌生人到來，他有行李放在車站，明天早上你該好好看看那些行李裝了什麼。」泰迪警告他。

「你們全都別説了，」霍爾太太厲聲吼：「管好自己的事就好了。」

但是霍爾太太對這名陌生人起了很大的疑心。

`p. 20-21` 隔天早上，霍爾先生將那名神祕男子的行李帶回旅館。

「我的天啊！」霍爾太太驚訝地大喊：「他到底有多少箱子和袋子啊？」

陌生人走出來，開始幫忙從運貨馬車上卸下東西。就在這個時候，一隻狗跑過來對著陌生人吼叫，還咬他的腿。這名男子看了看自己被咬破的衣服，然後很快地走回他的房間。

「我去看看他有沒有事。」霍爾先生説。他走進去時，發現男子的門開著。當他正要開口説話時，看到了非常令人吃驚的景象：男子外套的袖子在空中揮舞著，但裡面卻沒有手！突然間，霍爾先生感覺到自己被粗暴地推出房間，接著就是很大一聲「砰！」，門應聲關了起來。

霍爾先生感到很困惑。

「我有沒有看錯？」他問自己。

現在已經有一小群人聚集起來，大家都在討論狗攻擊陌生人的事。「他需要有人幫他看看咬傷的地方。」群眾中有人這麼説。「嗯，可是我沒看到他流血。」另一個人説。這時，陌生人又出現了，他穿著新的衣服。

「先生，你有沒有受傷？」霍爾太太問。

「完全沒有。」他回答。

`p. 22-23` 終於，男子所有的行李都被帶去他的房間了。他很快打開行李，拿出他的設備開始工作。他工作了一早上，到了午餐時間，霍爾太太將午餐送去給他。她敲敲門，但男子沒有回應，她便直接走了進去。而這時，男子沒有戴著眼鏡，而他的眼窩竟然是空的。

「我的天啊！」她倒抽一口氣。

男子聽到了她的聲音，很快地戴上眼鏡。「妳不應該沒敲門就進來。」他生氣地說。

「可是我確實有敲門。」她說。

「不准打擾我，我必須要全神貫注才行。」

「好的，先生。」霍爾太太回答。「門上有個鎖，我建議你使用它。」

然後霍爾太太就離開了。

下午其餘的時間，男子都在他房裡安靜地工作。但是，霍爾太太卻突然聽到瓶子摔破的聲音，以及沈重的腳步聲。她很快上樓去，卻因為太害怕而不敢敲門，只是在門外聽。

「這是不可能的！」她聽到男子說：「照這樣下去，我永遠不可能完成這項實驗。這會花上一輩子的時間！我沒有這種耐性！」

p. 24–25 有好幾個禮拜，陌生人都在他的房間裡工作。他通常很安靜，但偶爾發怒時，會砸壞家具和他的設備。在極少數的情況下，他會在傍晚出去散步，這時他總是把自己包得緊緊的，忽略村莊裡的人對他表達友善的舉動。霍爾先生提議要把陌生人趕走，但是霍爾太太說：「他一直都有付清帳單，附加費用也有付。我們還有這麼多空房間，不能太挑剔。」

陌生人成為村民間普遍的話題。許多人都相信泰迪・亨佛瑞所說的，認為這名男子在逃亡。

有一個人對這名陌生人特別好奇，他是村莊裡的醫生——強・古斯。他聽說了那些數以千計的瓶瓶罐罐，因此很想見他。

有一天，他找到了一個拜訪這陌生人的好理由：他要請他捐款作為護士基金。霍爾太太帶他去陌生人的房間。古斯醫生敲敲門，進入了房間，期間霍爾太太在外面等。十分鐘之後，房裡傳出很大的跺腳聲以及陣陣的笑聲，接著，門很快地被打開了。臉被嚇得慘白的古斯醫生跑出房間；在他身後，還能聽見陌生人詭異的笑聲。

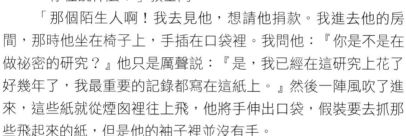

p.26–27 古斯醫生從旅館逃出來，一路跑到邦亭教士的家。他急忙衝進去見教士，教士感到很困惑。

「我會瘋掉！」他大喊。

「你在說什麼？」教士問。

「那個陌生人啊！我去見他，想請他捐款。我進去他的房間，那時他坐在椅子上，手插在口袋裡。我問他：『你是不是在做祕密的研究？』他只是厲聲說：『是，我已經在這研究上花了好幾年了，我最重要的記錄都寫在這紙上。』然後一陣風吹了進來，這些紙就從煙囪裡往上飛，他將手伸出口袋，假裝要去抓那些飛起來的紙，但是他的袖子裡並沒有手。

我問他：『你的手呢？』他站起來走向我，真是令人毛骨悚然！他把臉湊到我的面前，舉起他的手臂，這時，我看到一只空袖子往我的臉伸過來，接下來就感覺到一根手指和拇指捏了我的鼻子！」

此時，教士笑了出來。「古斯，你有喝酒嗎？」他問這名醫生。

「不！沒有！你一定要相信我，我甚至還揮動我的手臂，撞到了他的空袖子，感覺上就像撞到一隻手臂一樣。我說的都是實話！他就像鬼一樣！」

## [第二章] 令人困惑的搶案

p. 30-31 大約過了一個月後，五月的某天早上，邦亭太太聽到她臥室的窗外傳來聲響。

「醒醒！醒醒！」她對著還在睡覺的丈夫，也就是那位教士，低聲說：「有人在房子裡！」

教士起來，從壁爐裡拿出一根火鉗，悄悄地走到走廊上。他聽到樓下傳出打噴嚏的聲音。邦亭教士和他的太太慢慢走下樓梯，這時他們聽到書房裡紙張沙沙作響的聲音。

他們來到門口往裡面瞧，看到本來應該一片黑暗的房間，現在卻被一根蠟燭照亮了。在光亮中，他們看到有個抽屜被打開了，但房間裡卻沒有竊賊的蹤跡。突然間，傳來「叮！叮！」的聲音。

「他搜到了我們的錢。」邦亭太太低聲說：「一共有兩千多英鎊呀！」

p. 32-33 教士此時非常生氣，他衝進去大喊：「我抓到你了！投降吧！」

邦亭太太從她丈夫身後衝進去，他們兩人都驚訝得啞口無言。

「但是房間裡是空的！」教士大叫。

「聽！」他太太驚聲喊：「有人在這裡，我可以聽到呼吸的聲音。」

他們搜索了整個房間，卻找不到人。

「一定有人來過這裡。燈被點亮了，而且我們的錢也不見了。」

「哈——啾！」打噴嚏的聲音從走廊傳來，邦亭夫婦趕緊跑去看看有誰在那兒。他們衝到走廊，卻只聽到廚房的門猛然關閉的聲音。他們跑過去，很快將門打開，卻還是什麼人也沒看到。

在這起竊案發生後不久，霍爾夫婦醒來，並且發現他們旅館前門的門鎖被打開了。

p. 34–35 「我確定我昨天晚上有鎖門的。」霍爾太太説。

「除了他，還有誰會這麼做？」霍爾先生指著那名陌生人的房間説。

他們上去那名男子的房間，敲了敲門，卻沒有回應。

「我們進去吧。」霍爾太太説。他們開門進去時，房間裡卻沒看到人。「房間是空的，可是他的衣服全都在這裡。還有，看看這些繃帶。」霍爾太太評論著。「他的床是冷的，這表示他已經起來一陣子了。」

就在這個時刻，怪異的事發生了。所有的床單都自己捲在一起，然後跳過床鋪；接著，陌生人的帽子騰空飛過來，打到霍爾太太的臉；空中還傳來一陣可怕的邪惡笑聲。接著，他們看到一張扶手椅在空中向他們移動。

霍爾太太尖叫了起來，並感覺到自己被推出房間，她的丈夫就在她前面一起被推出去。然後門猛然關閉，門閂鎖了起來。霍爾太太對丈夫説：「他跟魔鬼做交易，那裡面有邪惡的靈魂。」

「一定有別的解釋才對。」她的丈夫説。

p. 36–37 「我要他離開我的旅館，他把邪惡的靈魂放到家具裡面去了。」霍爾太太説。

突然間，他們聽到樓梯頂端有個聲音。

「不准進去我的房間，你們沒有權利進去那裡。」陌生人對他們大吼。這時，霍爾夫婦盯著彼此看。「這怎麼可能？我們才剛進去過，他不在裡面啊，他怎麼能……？」霍爾太太抽了一口氣。

　　但是接下來的早上，他們都沒有見到陌生人。事實上，當他按鈴時，他們甚至還未加以理會。

　　到了中午時，大家都聽説了邦亭家裡發生的竊盜案。所有的老顧客都在酒吧，談論著關於搶案的八卦。就在酒吧內一片喧囂時，大家的談話突然都停了下來。

　　陌生人走進酒吧，盤問説：「你們為什麼沒有拿早餐來給我，又為什麼不回應我的門鈴？」

　　「你沒有付帳單，沒付錢就沒食物和房間。」霍爾太太生氣地回答。

　　「我跟妳説過，我幾天之內就會給妳了。錢在這裡。」

　　「喔，這可有趣了。你怎麼得到這些錢的？你還要解釋你對我的家具做了什麼，還有，你怎麼能不經過門就進到自己的房間。」她盤問他。

`p. 38-39` 這使得男子非常生氣。「別説了！妳懂什麼。」他大吼。「那好，我就讓妳看看。」男子將手放在臉上，然後將一個小小的橡膠似的東西，放到她手上。

　　「看！那是他的鼻子！他臉上有個洞！」所有人都驚叫起來。接著，男子將眼鏡和臉上所有的東西都拔下來；突然間，這名穿著長外套的男子沒有了頭。這時大家全都歇斯底里了起來，紛紛跑出旅館。大家對於目睹這樣的事情，一點心理準備都沒有。

　　霍爾太太説：「他是個邪惡的靈魂。」

　　有個警察聽到了這陣騷動，便過來問：「這裡到底發生了什麼事？」

　　「有個無頭男子在旅館裡。」霍爾先生告訴他。「好的，」警察説：「我去逮捕他。」

霍爾先生和警察走進旅館。這名旅館主人指著那個沒有頭的身體，說：「就是他。」

陌生人現在生氣地問：「你以為你在做什麼？」

p. 40–41 警察說：「我要逮捕你。」

「離我遠一點。」陌生人警告他。

這名警察往陌生人走過去。這時，陌生人已經拿下了一隻手套，並用拳頭毆打這名警察。

「抓住他的腿！」警察大喊。霍爾先生試著要抓住他的腿，但是這名陌生人卻重重地打了他。警察終於勉強將陌生人推倒在地上。

「我放棄了。」陌生人說。他站起來，很快地開始將衣服都脫掉。警察和霍爾先生兩個人，看到一個穿著衣服的身體彎腰將鞋子脫下來，但是他卻沒有腳。

霍爾先生驚呼：「他不是人，他的衣服裡根本沒有東西！」他將手伸出去，看看能不能摸到這名男子，但這時卻傳來一聲尖叫：「好痛！你戳到我的眼睛了！我是人，只是我是隱形的，但這並不代表你們就有權利逮捕我，或是戳我的眼睛。」

警察接著說：「我是為了邦亭家的竊盜案要逮捕你。」但這時男子已經將鞋子、襪子和褲子都脫下來了。他們看到的，只有一件上衣在房間裡跑來跑去。

p. 42–43 就在伊坪村外，一名流浪漢，湯瑪斯・馬佛，坐著看著兩雙鞋子，想決定要穿哪一雙鞋。他正盯著靴子看時，身後有個聲音說：「兩雙鞋都很醜。」

「是啊。」流浪漢説。「我該穿哪一雙好呢？」然後，他轉頭問：「你穿什麼鞋？」

但是他才問完，就發現身後並沒有人。「我一定是瘋了。」他大聲説。

「不，你沒有瘋。」他後面的聲音説。

「你在哪裡？」流浪漢問。「我一定是喝醉了，或是在自言自語。」

「不，別擔心，你沒有喝醉。」

流浪漢再次四處環顧，感到非常困惑。「我確定自己有聽到聲音。」

就在這時，某個東西抓住馬佛的衣領，搖晃著他。

「你不是在幻想。」這個聲音説：「我是個隱形人。」

這時，馬佛説：「我是個流浪漢，但不是笨蛋，沒人能隱形的。」

p. 44-45 就在這個時候，流浪漢感覺到有東西抓住他的手，於是他往後跳。接著，馬佛將手伸出去，觸摸那隻抓住他的手，而他感覺到自己摸到手臂、胸膛，然後是鬍子。

「這真是太驚人了！」流浪漢説。「這怎麼可能呢？」

「我晚點再告訴你。」隱形人説：「現在，我需要你的幫助。這個社會拒絕了我們兩個，所以我們應該要互相幫助。」

「我要怎麼幫助你呢？」馬佛問。

「先從衣服和棲身處開始吧。我也能幫助你。你能想像我有什麼力量嗎？如果你背叛我，我會做出很可怕的事情。」

流浪漢此時感到很害怕。「好的，我……我不會背叛你的。」他結結巴巴地説。「別擔心，我會幫助你的。」

在伊坪村裡，事情已經全部平靜下來了。人們一方面對於這個怪人的存在感到懷疑，一方面又因他的離開而放下心。而大約下午四點時，一個流浪漢進入村莊，直接走到陌生人的房間。

p. 46–47 流浪漢看到兩個人，古斯醫生和邦亭教士，在翻三本很大的書。

「這是某種密碼。」古斯醫生説。

「你們在做什麼？」流浪漢問。這兩人抬頭看，看到是個流浪漢，都鬆了一口氣。

「酒吧在下面。」醫生説。

「謝謝你。」馬佛回答。他下樓去喝了杯酒，然後走出去，在隱形人的房間下面等。

這兩人在臥室裡翻看著那些書時，突然間感覺到有又冷又尖鋭的東西頂在脖子上。

「我不想傷害你們，但你們讓我沒有選擇。」一個熟悉的聲音説：「你們有什麼權利看我的私人物品？我的衣服又在哪裡？」

「霍爾太太拿走了。」

「很好，那我只要……」

「不要！」醫生和教士同時大喊。幾分鐘後，一捆書飛出窗外，被流浪漢接住。對街一家店的店主，杭斯特先生，看到了這一幕，大喊：「停！小偷！」他開始追著流浪漢跑，卻感覺到自己臉上被揍了一拳，接著就倒在地上，不省人事。

p. 48–49 一段時間過後，古斯醫生跑下旅館的樓梯。他大喊：「他拿了我的褲子，還有教士身上所有的衣服！阻止他！」

在他身後，教士跑了出來，用一條毯子和一份日報遮住身體。這兩個人在街道上奔跑著，結果絆到昏倒在地的杭斯特先生而跌倒。其他人都跑過來看這陣混亂是怎麼回事；就在這個時候，大家紛紛被摔倒在地上，或是臉上挨了拳頭。所有人都在驚嚇中跑走了。

然而，隱形人還是很生氣。他回到鎮上，開始破壞所有東西：他用斧頭將霍爾先生的手推車砍得肢離破碎；他去古斯醫生的辦公室，將裡面所有的東西都砸壞；他將街燈甩進窗戶裡，還切斷電報的電線。

在隱形人的盛怒過去了之後，他離開了伊坪，之後就再也沒有人看到、聽到，或是感覺到他的存在了。

## p. 52–53 維爾斯的科幻故事主題

H・G・維爾斯是個社會主義的思考者，他也對科學發展的神奇很感興趣。他最著名的小說之一《時光機器》就同時探討了以上兩個主題。

在這本小說中，維爾斯發明了一種時光機器，並描寫了資本階級結構的自然演化。故事中，一個稱為「伊羅依」的人類社會，代表著富有的社會高階，他們擁有一切所需的東西，卻對生活失去興趣。維爾斯很可能並不認為像這樣的社會階層確實存在，但在他對伊羅依社會的描寫中，的確提出了一些有趣的想法。

維爾斯的許多小說現在稱為科幻小說，這主要是因為這些書的情節，都著重在科學發現帶來的衝擊。維爾斯會對科學這麼感興趣，並非巧合。十八世紀末，科學知識有很大的進展，工業化的過程在社會上造成了很大的改變，許多人都好奇未來會變得如何：有些人認為未來會是天堂，認為科學的進步會創造一個完美的社會；有些人則認為由於富人利用貧人，人類文明將會退化，並遭受可怕的毀滅。

## [ 第三章 ] 不速之客

p. 54–55　在伊坪鎮外好幾哩遠之處，湯馬斯·馬佛沿著路，帶著三本厚重的書沈重地走著。他四處環顧，想找機會逃跑，但隱形人總是在這時候對他說：「如果你逃跑，我會找到你，然後殺了你。」

「可是我很弱的，我沒辦法幫你。」流浪漢說。

「你最好照我的話去做。大家都會尋找我的下落，所以我需要你幫我完成我做不到的事。」隱形人說：「你最好保護我的書不受損害，如果你沒做到，我會殺了你。」

他們走了許多個小時，終於在早上抵達了史多港。他們一直等到銀行開門後，隱形人就走進銀行，馬佛則在外面等。突然間，一捆捆的錢從窗戶飛出來，馬佛很快地把錢裝進外套和褲子的口袋裡，接著就一直逃跑，直到他喘不過氣來為止。

他找到一個座位坐下來，將三本書放在他旁邊。不久之後，一名老水手在他旁邊坐下，他拿了一份報紙，說：「看看這個！這上面寫說有個隱形人在這些地方活動。」

p. 56–57　馬佛疑神疑鬼地環顧四周。他仔細聽著是否有隱形人的聲音，但什麼都沒聽到，所以他就對這名水手低聲說：「我知道一些關於這個隱形人的事。」

水手十分吃驚，問道：「真的嗎？你知道些什麼？」

「呃，我⋯⋯好痛！」流浪漢呻吟了起來。現在他把手放在左耳旁邊。原來隱形人用手掌打了他的側腦。「是⋯⋯呃⋯⋯是我的⋯⋯呃⋯⋯牙齒，我有嚴重的牙痛。我現在要走了。」

「那關於隱形人的事呢？」水手在流浪漢身後大喊。

「那不是真的，一切都是某個我認識的人編出來的故事。」流浪漢一邊說，一邊被隱形人沿著馬路拖著走。

馬佛和隱形人離開了史多港，前往距離很近的博達克港。在這個鎮上，亞瑟・凱普博士正在書房裡，透過顯微鏡看東西。他是個研究科學家。

p. 58–59 凱普博士決定休息一下，便站起來走到窗邊。透過窗戶，他看到一個外表髒兮兮的男子邊揮著手，邊在街上跑著。「又是個瘋瘋癲癲的笨蛋，在那喊著關於隱形人的事。為什麼鎮上這麼多這種人？」

但那些近距離看到馬佛的人，並不認為他瘋了，尤其他們還聽到馬佛身後有粗重的呼吸聲。有兩個男孩突然被推倒在地，還有隻狗被一條看不到的腿踢開。

大家驚慌了起來，紛紛離開街上，有些人甚至還邊跑邊尖叫：「隱形人來了！」然而，在「快活板球員」旅館中，一切都很正常。當常客們正在享用平常喝的酒時，馬佛從門口闖進來，大叫：「隱形人在追我，快把門鎖上！他說過如果我逃走，他會殺了我！」

一個警察說：「快點！把門鎖上！」

他們才剛將門閂上，就聽到門上傳來強力的重擊聲。

「不要開門！」馬佛驚恐地喊：「所有的門都鎖上了嗎？」

「後門！還有後院的門！」酒保驚聲喊道。

p. 60–61 酒保匆匆忙忙跑去檢查門，但已經太遲了。「後院的門是開的，他現在可能已經進來了。」他告訴大家。接著就傳來甩門的聲音。酒保伸手拿起一把刀子，警察也伸手拿他的槍。突然，不知從哪裡來的某樣東西，把馬佛從他躲藏的地方拖出來。

隱形人將馬佛拖到廚房裡，警察跟上去試著要抓住隱形人，但他感覺到一個偌大的拳頭往臉上打過來。酒保和警察兩人都試圖要抓住隱形人。當隱形人在擊退這兩人時，馬佛成功地爬走，帶著那三本書從後院的門逃走了。

扭打持續了一陣子後，這兩人發覺自己已經感覺不到隱形人的存在了。

「他在哪裡？」其中一人問。

「他一定逃走了。」另一人説。

就在這個時候，一個盤子從空中飛了過來；警察對著盤子飛過來的地方射了五槍。

「你可能射到他了。我們試著摸摸看他的身體在哪。」

p. 62–63 在城鎮的另一頭，凱普博士在忙著做研究。在打鬥發生時，他正在寫下一些筆記；當他聽到槍聲時，他抬起頭想：「嗯，今晚在『快活板球員』裡又在打架了。」

他回到工作上，但此時門鈴響了。過了一段時間，還是沒人進來書房見他，於是他將他的女管家叫來。

「剛剛是誰來？」他問。

「沒有人。」她告訴他：「一定是有人惡作劇。」

之後凱普博士就忘了這件事，繼續工作到凌晨兩點。這時他決定上床睡覺，所以就上去他的房間。

就在他進房間之前，他看到地板上有像血的東西；然後他看看門把，發現門把上覆蓋著泥巴。他走進臥室，看到被單上都是血；接著他仔細看看他的枕頭。「天啊！看起來像是有人曾經躺在這裡過！」他大叫。

就在這個時候，房間裡有另一個聲音說：「凱普，是你！我真不敢相信！」

凱普博士環顧房間，看到在角落有看起來像是沾了血的繃帶，包裹在看不到的手臂上。

p. 64–65 「別擔心，凱普，我是隱形人，你並沒有幻聽。」

「什麼？隱形人？所以村子裡的人說的是真的！」凱普博士說著，伸出手去摸那圈繃帶，但隱形人抓住了博士的手腕；凱普博士試著將手拉開並反抗，但隱形人說：「凱普，別這樣！你認識我的，我是傑克‧葛林芬。我們一起上大學的。」

這時，凱普坐起來問：「那個贏得大學化學獎章的傑克‧葛林芬？」

「是的。」

「為什麼你會想讓自己隱形？」凱普博士又問：「你又是怎麼做到的？」

隱形人回答：「凱普，我可以明天再解釋嗎？我現在受了傷，精疲力盡，肚子又很餓。我可以喝點東西嗎？」凱普博士倒了些威士忌給他，問：「你在哪裡？」

葛林芬從他手中拿走杯子。「我不敢相信這一切會是真的。」凱普博士說。

「我在外頭沒穿衣服奔走好一陣子了。我只想要穿上一些乾淨的衣服，吃點東西。」凱普博士走到衣櫥，拿出一件浴袍，說：「這個可以嗎？」

隱形人拿走那件浴袍。凱普博士看著那件浴袍，它看起來就像是自己在空中擺盪著。博士也拿了些內衣、襪子和拖鞋給他，接著去拿一些食物。他帶了食物回來，然後看著那張隱形的嘴巴狼吞虎嚥地吃下去。

`p. 66–67`「這真是怪事。」他喃喃地說。
　　「奇怪的是我竟然這麼好運，為了找包紮傷口的繃帶，竟然就進了一個舊識的屋子裡。」葛林芬說。
　　「你怎麼受傷的？」博士說。
　　「唔，有個本來應該要幫助我的人，他叫馬佛。」
　　「他用槍射你？」博士又問他。
　　「不，但他偷了我的書和錢。」
　　「你有拿槍射他嗎？我聽到旅館那邊傳來槍聲。」
　　「不，是某個在旅館裡的人射傷我，但我晚點再解釋，我累了。」
　　「那就在我房裡睡一覺吧。」博士提議說。
　　「睡覺？我得抓到馬佛，拿回我的書！還有，警察可能會來抓我。」男子說。
　　「警察？」凱普問。
　　「我真是個笨蛋！我竟然讓你想到可以把我交給警察。」
　　「我答應你我不會這麼做的，我不會告訴任何人你在這裡。你何不在我走後鎖上門呢？」凱普博士建議道。
　　「好吧，那我今晚就在這裡睡。我明天會向你解釋我的計畫，我們可以一起做些很棒的事情。我剛發現如果我要當隱形人，我一定要有個搭檔才行。」
　　這兩人握手互道晚安，但隱形人此時警告他：「你最好不要想著要讓我被抓到。」

## [第四章] 一個驚人的發現

p. 70–71 凱普博士離開房間後，聽到隱形人將門鎖上的聲音。

「我一定是瘋了，這一切不可能是真的。」他心想：「不！這全是真的。」

他靜靜地走下樓到他的辦公室去，然後找出當天的報紙，開始尋找一些文章。他讀的第一篇標題叫做「伊坪的奇異故事」；另一篇的名稱是「蘇斯克斯整座村都瘋了」。他讀到一些關於人們被攻擊的事件：有個醫生和教士被脫掉衣服，還有些建築物被摧毀。

凱普博士心想：「這個人既瘋狂又危險，他能殺人呀。」

凱普博士憂心忡忡，整夜都沒睡，一直想著自己該怎麼做。到了早上，他的女管家過來，他請她準備兩份早餐，放在他的書房裡。在他的辦公室裡，他讀了早報，上面描述了前一晚發生的事件。這時凱普博士更憂心了，他坐下來寫了一張紙條，收件人寫「艾達上校，布達克港口警方」。就在他要把紙條交給女管家時，他聽到家具被砸壞的聲音。

「快一點。」他低聲對女管家說。

p. 72–73 凱普博士跑上樓敲門。「怎麼了？」他問那件無頭的浴袍。

「我發了頓脾氣。」隱形人解釋道。

「你好像常常這樣。報紙上都是你的消息，但沒人知道你在這裡。」

隱形人似乎非常激動，於是凱普博士建議道：「我們到我書房裡吃早餐好嗎？」

　　這個建議讓葛林芬的心情好了一些，他們就前往書房。凱普博士緊張地往窗戶外看，然後在他隱形的夥伴對面坐了下來。

　　「葛林芬，我很想知道這一切是怎麼發生在你身上的。」凱普博士說。

　　「起初一切都很美好，但現在我遇到了這麼多問題，我不確定是不是真的那麼好了，除非我能做到什麼了不起的事情。讓我告訴你我的故事吧。」葛林芬說：「如你所知，我們在許多年前一起研究藥品，但你知道在那之後，我轉而研究物理學嗎？我對光線和液體做了許多研究，還研究當光線穿過在水中的玻璃時，玻璃幾乎是隱形的現象。」

p. 74–75 「是的，但人類並不像玻璃那樣是透明的。」凱普打斷他的話。

　　「不，其實我們是透明的，除了我們血液中的紅色素和其他物質之外。我們的肉體、骨頭、指甲、頭髮，一切都是透明的。六年來，我做了許多研究，並且把所有結果都寫在我的三本書裡，這就是為什麼我一定要從馬佛那裡把書拿回來。」

　　「但你是怎麼讓血液和其他顏色變得隱形的？」凱普問。

　　「我花了三年多才做到這件事，但我一直都沒有錢，所以我從我父親那裡偷了錢。但那之後他舉槍自盡了，因為我偷的錢原來就是他欠別人的錢。唉，我用這筆錢買了所有需要的設備，所以就開始有能力讓一些東西隱形了。

　　首先，我把一片木頭變得隱形；然後我找到了一隻餓肚子的貓，我拿了摻了藥的食物給牠吃，幾小時之後，這隻貓慢慢開始隱形。牠失去意識很長一段時間，當牠終於醒來時，我只能看

到她眼睛裡的綠色。我最後一次看到牠時，牠看起來只是一對從我窗口跳出去的綠眼睛。」

p. 76–77 「在成功地讓這隻貓隱形之後，我就知道要讓人類隱形，確實是有可能的。我努力研究，而且我得快點成功才行，因為我欠房東一大筆房租，我知道如果我能隱形起來，就此消失，一切就能完美解決。我決定把那三本書寄到倫敦的另一地址給自己。

在從郵局回來之後，我幫自己混合了一些藥劑喝了下去。當我在等它發揮作用時，有人敲我的門。這時我覺得很不舒服，而當我開門時，我的房東看著我，尖叫著跑走了。我看看鏡子裡的自己，發現我白得跟紙一樣。

接下來的十到十二個小時之間，我承受難以言喻的痛苦。到早上的時候，我慢慢變隱形了。我看著鏡子裡的自己，當然其實什麼都看不到，而這時門上傳來一聲巨響，是我的房東。他大喊著要我開門。我十分絕望，我不想讓別人看到我的藥品和設備，所以只好燒了那間房子，並從窗戶逃走。

p. 78–79 「我決定前往我寄送書的地方。隱形一開始很有趣，但也有不少問題。我不能穿任何衣服和鞋子，這讓我非常冷，我的腳也很痛。狗和小男孩也是個問題。狗看不到我，但是牠們當然可以聞到我的味道。當我走過水坑或泥坑時，小男孩總會大喊：『看！那邊有腳印，可是沒有人走在上面。』這時我身後就會出現人群，我就得試圖找到某些完全乾的地面，好逃離那裡。最後我好不容易才擺脫那群追捕者。」

在聽到「追捕者」這個詞時，凱普覺得有點不自在。他緊張地從窗戶往外瞥了一下。

隱形人繼繼說他的故事：「那天，我明白我得趕快找到一個棲身之處。接下來一定會下雪，而我知道如果雪落在我身上，人們就能輕易看到我。」

p. 80–81 「我找到一間百貨公司，一直等到看門人為顧客打開門後，便趕緊進去。我找到一個可以休息的角落，當店打烊時，我找了一些食物吃，還找來一些衣服穿上。我打算在那裡睡，從收銀機偷些錢，然後完成我的偽裝。問題是我睡得太熟了，我沒有在店開門之前醒來，所以有許多人看到我。我跳起來趕快逃跑，但我當時看起來就是個無頭人，在店裡跑來跑去，所以我躲在某個櫃台後面，把身上的衣服全都扯下來；我好不容易在警察剛到達時逃脫。

　　我當時很餓，但是不能吃東西，因為如果我沒穿衣服，人們就能看到我胃裡的食物。」隱形人繼續說。

　　「嗯，我從來沒想到這個問題。」凱普評論說：「那外頭的雪怎麼辦？」

　　「到了早上，雪全都融化了。但天氣非常的冷，我必須儘快找到衣服來穿。我可以感覺到自己快生病了。」

p. 82–83 「我匆匆在街上找，終於找到一間小小的戲服店，它藏在一條小街道上，所以沒有人在那附近。我靜靜地進入商店；店主聽到我進去，他什麼也沒看到，所以就回去後面吃午餐──至少我是這麼以為的。但那男人又回來了，而且手上還拿了一把槍。他大喊：『誰在那裡？我知道有人在，我有聽到你進來的聲音。』接著他就開槍了，但是沒有打中我。這時我知道我得採取極端的手段了。」

　　「什麼？你殺了他，是不是？」凱普問。

　　「不！不！我當時並沒有這種想法。我拿了一張小凳子，打他的後腦，他失去了意識，然後我就拿東西塞住他的嘴，再用床單將他綁住，還蓋住他的頭，這樣如果他醒來了，也看不到我穿上偽裝裝扮的樣子。凱普！我希望你不要那樣看我。我一定得這麼做的，我沒有選擇，他有槍啊！接著我拿了些眼鏡、一頂假髮、一些假鬍子，還有那個人櫃台收銀機裡所有的錢，之後就離開了。」

p. 84–85 「我接下來所做的，就是弄點東西來吃。我找到一間餐廳，它有私人的用餐室。我向侍者解釋，說我不想在公眾場合吃東西，因為我被毀容了。」

這個時候，隱形人停下談話。他似乎轉了過來，面對著正在窗戶前來回踱步的凱普。博士不想讓葛林芬起疑心，所以他試著讓他繼續說話。

「你就是在那時候去伊坪的嗎？」博士問隱形人。

「是的。」他回答：「那就是我把書寄達的地點，連同我的衣服和設備一起。我想住在一個安靜的小村莊裡，這樣就不會有人來打擾我了。我想靜靜地研究，配出一份能讓我的身體能再被看見的處方。我想再恢復成別人看得到的模樣，但在那之前，我想先趁隱形時做我想做的事，這件事我需要你的幫忙，凱普。」

「我不會幫助你犯那些你至今所犯過的罪。」凱普回答：「你已經攻擊好幾個人了。」

「他們不會有任何問題的，除了湯瑪斯‧馬佛之外。當我追上他時，他會希望自己從來沒出生在這世上。我也會殺了任何想阻止我實現計畫的人。」

p. 88–89 **真的隱形了**

如果你能隱形一天，你會做什麼？ H‧G‧維爾斯和其他探索過這個想法的作家，都描寫了一個隱形人可能擁有的驚人力量。他們可以暗中到任何地方，並且偷取錢財或貴重物品。

然而，這些作者似乎都忽略了一點，那就是如果一個人真的隱形了，他將會看不見！視覺只有在眼睛能捕捉光線時，才能發揮作用。如果眼球的後方是透明的，光線將會直接穿越眼球，這樣眼睛就無法傳送影像到大腦。那你能想像一個也失去視力的隱形人會如何嗎？

在維爾斯這本小說見市將近一百年後，科學上最接近隱形人的成就，是「隱密裝」。這種服裝現在仍在研發中，它是由畫素組成的，就像是可以拿來穿著的電腦螢幕。這些畫素會與穿著這套服裝的士兵背後任何顏色相同。這並不能算是真正的隱形，比較像是變色龍那樣，配合所在的背景，改變皮膚的顏色；然而，這卻是保證不用失去視力，又能隱形的最好方法了！

## ［第五章］叛徒！

p. 90–91 正當葛林芬在告訴凱普他的計畫時，凱普注意到有三個人往他的房子走過來。他從窗邊走開，站在窗戶和隱形人的中間。

「你打算在這裡做什麼？」

「我原本的計畫是去西班牙，那裡的天氣熱，我就可以不用穿著衣服行走了。」

「那是個好主意，你什麼時候要離開？」凱普問。

「既然我突然遇上了你，我不打算離開了。你是個科學家，沒有人比你更能完全了解我這了不起的發現了。你比那個搶奪我一切的流浪漢，更能幫得上忙。」

到了這個地步，凱普變得極度擔心。

「你……你是不是……最……最好先從他那裡……把書拿回來呢？」凱普結結巴巴地說：「我在報上看到他請警方將他鎖在監獄裡。」

「我會抓到他的。相信我，我會的。」隱形人做出保證。他發出一種笑聲，使他顯得完全瘋狂了。

p. 92–93 很幸運的，他的笑聲掩蓋過了有人從前門進屋裡去的聲音。

「我們可以做任何事，凱普。我們可以偷竊！我們可以殺人！我們可以懲罰任何想阻止我們的人。」葛林芬狂熱地說。

「但是，雖然你是隱形的，我卻不是。」凱普說：「你為什麼要我把自己置於這樣的危險中？我已經給了你……」

「噓！那是什麼聲音？」葛林芬說。

「我沒聽到什麼聲音。」

凱普下定決心，絕對不要讓葛林芬知道已經有一些人進了屋子。「我不可能幫助你進行你的計畫。我認為你應該把你的研究公開發表，讓全世界其他的人看到。我會幫你研究出可以讓你恢復正常的處方；也許我們可以再找一位科學家來幫忙。」

葛林芬再度打斷他：「腳步聲！他們上樓來了。你最好沒有告訴任何人我在這裡，如果你說了的話……」葛林芬警告他。

「我沒告訴任何人。」

葛林芬開始往門的方向走，但凱普擋住他。

「叛徒！你背叛了我。」隱形人大叫。

p. 94–95 這時，隱形人開始將浴袍脫下來。凱普伸手將門猛力打開，葛林芬試圖要跟上他，但凱普將他推回房間裡。他想將隱形人鎖在房間裡，但當門用力甩上時，鑰匙掉了出來。

凱普非常用力地擋著門，但葛林芬努力將門拉開了一點。

體擠進門和門框之間，他伸出隱形的手，用手指抓住凱普的喉嚨；凱普的手從門把上鬆開，接著一件騰空飛舞的浴袍就跑出來到走廊上。一轉眼，這件浴袍就將凱普壓倒在樓梯頂端的地上了。

在樓梯中間，驚愕的警長艾達上校看著凱普和一件瘋狂扭動的浴袍扭打。接著，上校看到一件浴袍就在他的面前；突然間，他感覺到尖銳的指甲刺進他的喉嚨，同時隱形人用膝蓋頂撞他的胃部，使他感覺到肚子一陣劇烈的疼痛；下一刻他清醒時，就倒在樓梯的底部了。

「我們追丟他了！」凱普大叫，他滿臉是血。

p. 96–97 過了好幾分鐘，這幾個人才定下心神來。凱普帶領上校進辦公室，他們一起喝了杯酒。

「那個人瘋了，他已經完全失去了理智。如果我們不阻止他，他會殺很多人。」凱普說。

「我們一定要抓到他，也一定會的。」上校回答。

「我們得趁他在這一帶時抓到他。他想從馬佛那裡拿回他的書，那是唯一將他留在這裡的理由。所有的屋子都一定要上鎖。我們得阻止他睡覺、吃東西或拿衣服。」

上校同意凱普說的話。「對。你得和我一起來，幫忙組織搜查。你對他最了解。」

「好的。」凱普同意：「我們也該用狗來幫忙，牠們看不到他，卻可以聞到他的味道。還有，告訴你的手下，要他們把武器藏起來。他會試著使用任何他找得到的武器。」

上校仔細聽凱普的話。「好的。還有別的嗎？」

「有，在路上放滿碎玻璃，那會割傷他的腳。」

p. 98–99 這兩人就此離開，去組織追捕隱形人的行動。一到了下午，整個國家就都知道關於這名危險隱形人的事了。到處都貼了警告，學校關閉了，所有的建築和房屋都鎖了起來。整個博多克港口的男人都配備了槍、刀子和棍棒等武器，狗都也都被放出來，試圖要找到隱形人的味道。

接下來幾天，有許多關於隱形人的傳聞。在離博多克港七、八哩遠的辛頓丁，有幾個人聲稱他們聽到奇怪的聲音經過一片田地，然後發出哭聲、笑聲、呻吟聲等等。

當艾達上校聽到這件事時，他對凱普說：「他一定是待在城外。他已經知道我們現在都將屋子鎖上，並嚴加戒備了。」

「對，但他已經絕望了。希望他會做些什麼蠢事，讓我們找到他。」凱普說。

然而，隱形人卻有辦法躲避追捕；事實上，大家所不知道的是，隱形人變得越來越強了，而且更堅決地要保持自由之身。

p. 100–101 同一天稍晚，凱普博士在用午餐時，他的女管家拿了一封信給他，是從希頓丁寄來的。他很快打開信來看：

致博多克港的所有居民：

你們都很聰明，讓我在博多克港一帶難以生存。你們已經證明你們全都是和我對立的，你們會為此付出代價。我會開創一個恐怖統治的時代。告訴你們的艾達上校，博多克港的新統治者是隱形人。這個恐怖統治，會從凱普博士的處決開始。他也許躲起來，或是找來全世界的警衛來保護他，但我還是會殺了他。如果你們有誰幫助凱普博士，我會知道，而下一個死的就會是你。

凱普叫他的女管家過來。「請確認所有的窗戶和門隨時都是鎖住的。」他吩咐她，然後走上樓拿了槍。他非常生氣地大喊：「即使要拿我作餌，我們也一定要抓到他！」

他很快寫了一張紙條，拿給他的管家，要她拿去警察局。他告訴她：「待在警察局，除非我要求，不然不要回來這間房子。」

p. 102–103 管家離開了，但不到半個小時後，艾達上校到他家來了。

　　「是你的管家，」他說：「她說要幫你送一張紙條給我，但在她到警察局的路上，紙條從她的手中被奪走了。」

　　「喔，不！」凱普驚聲說：「我有個要抓住他的計畫，但現在被他知道那個計畫了！」

　　他們的對話被打破玻璃的聲音打斷了。

　　「現在他來了！他想要從臥室窗戶進來！」凱普大叫。

　　「很好，把你的槍給我，我去把追蹤犬帶過來。」艾達說。

　　凱普把槍拿給他，當他一離開，他更用力將門閂上。艾達走出房子，但這時他聽到身後有個聲音說：「不要動！」

　　就在這個時候，艾達感覺到背上一陣劇烈的疼痛，接著他就倒在地上。他感覺到槍被從手中搶走。他往上看，看到那把槍浮在半空中。

　　「如果不是還有更重要的事要做，我會殺了你。」那個聲音說：「站起來！」

　　艾達慢慢地站起來。

　　「現在，回到屋子裡去。」

　　「凱普不會讓我回去。」艾達說。

p. 104–105 凱普站在廚房的窗戶旁，看著一切的經過。他心想：「艾達應該開槍的。」但接著他看到槍飄在空中，才明白這是怎麼回事。他看到艾達往屋子走過來。突然間，艾達往後跳，試著抓住那把槍，接著傳來一聲槍聲，艾達就倒在地上了。凱普非常震驚。

他無法移動或思考，但木頭被撞裂的聲音讓他在廚房裡走動了一下。他從前面的窗戶往外看，看到兩名警官往他的屋子走來。他們按了門鈴，凱普讓他們進來。

「他有一把槍和斧頭。」凱普警告他們：「他任何時候都會進來。」

就在他拿給每個警官一人一把火鉗時，一把槍和斧頭出現在屋內。

一名警官成功地阻止了斧頭的攻擊，另一位警官則將槍從隱形人手中打掉；接下來，有人打中某個柔軟的東西，然後傳來痛苦的呻吟，斧頭也掉在地上。這名警官用火鉗打在同一個地方，但它只是重重地打在地上。

「他到哪裡去了？」一名警官問。「我不知道，我有打到他，但他一定逃走了。凱普博士也不見了。」另一名警官說。

p. 106–107 在他們打鬥的時候，凱普博士從一扇窗戶跳出去，前往他最近的鄰居家。他用力敲門，但因為人們很怕隱形人，所以沒人來開門。他決定找別的地方躲起來。他故意走在一條全是玻璃碎片的路上。

凱普往博多克港跑，但他可以聽到身後有腳步聲。

「隱形人！他在我背後！」他大叫。女人和小孩尖叫著逃跑，而鎮上的男人則紛紛拿起鏟子。

凱普大喊：「排成一排！」就在這時，有人從背後攻擊他，接著他感覺到有個拳頭打在下巴上。葛林芬抓住凱普的喉嚨，並用膝蓋頂他的胸口。

p. 108–109 當凱普試著要把葛林芬的手指從脖子上移開時，有把鏟子揮過空中，打中某個柔軟的東西。他喉嚨上的手指鬆開了，然後他感覺到葛林芬的身體就癱在他身上。

他還感覺到像血一樣濕濕的東西掉在臉上。「我抓到他了！」凱普大喊。一群男人跳到隱形人的身上，把他壓倒在地。

「拜託，拜託。」一個聲音呻吟說。

「放開他，放開他。」凱普命令道：「他受傷了。」

男子們離開他身上，凱普伸手尋找他的臉。

「我想他的臉上都是血。」凱普將手放在隱形人的胸口上，驚呼：「他沒有呼吸了！」

突然，聚集的人群中有個女人的聲音喊道：「看！」

每個人都往她手指的方向看去。葛林芬的其中一隻手上，血管和骨頭開始顯現出來了。

「他的腳也開始出現了。」另一個人喊道。這名男子的全身非常緩慢地開始重現。有個人從附近的一棟房子走出來，拿了一件床單，蓋在這名叫傑克‧葛林芬的三十歲男子的裸體上。

p. 110–111 這就是隱形人的結局；但他的故事還沒完全結束。有個居住在斯多港的有錢人，他曾經是個流浪漢，但現在他是一間旅館的主人。

對於那些拜訪旅館的人，他很樂意告訴他們關於隱形人的故事。他告訴他的客人，自己是如何智取那些想拿走他口袋裡的錢的警察，他還聲稱自己從來沒有看到傑克‧葛林芬寫的那三本筆記書。他說葛林芬把書藏到別的地方去了。但在有空的時候，這位湯瑪斯‧馬佛先生，會坐在他的書房裡，研究書裡奇怪的密碼。

「一旦我找出這些密碼的意義之後，我就能，唔，我絕對不會做他做的那些事。」

凱普和自槍傷復原的艾達上校，在許多不同的機會之下，詢問過馬佛關於書本的事，但直到馬佛辭世為止，沒有人知道這些書本的下落。

# Answers

P. 28
**A** ① (b)  ② (b)  ③ (a)  ④ (c)

**B** ① (b)  ② (c)  ③ (a)

P. 29
**C** ③ → ④ → ① → ⑤ → ②

**D** ① occasional  ② equipment  ③ covered
④ rid  ⑤ picky

P. 50
**A** ① -Mr. Bunting  ② -Mrs. Hall  ③ -the tramp
④ -the invisible man

**B** ① -e  ② -c  ③ -a  ④ -b  ⑤ -d

P. 51
**C** ① (a)  ② (b)  ③ (c)

**D** ① T  ② F  ③ F

P. 68
**A** ① (c)  ② (d)  ③ (a)  ④ (b)

**B** ① (b)  ② (b)

P. 69
**C** ① blood  ② covered  ③ closely  ④ voice

P. 86
**A** ① (c)  ② (b)  ③ (a)  ④ (c)

**B** ① about  ② to  ③ from  ④ on  ⑤ through

P. 87
**C** ① T  ② F  ③ F  ④ F  ⑤ T

**D** ② → ③ → ⑤ → ④ → ①

P. 112   (A)  **1** -b    **2** -a    **3** -c    **4** -e    **5** -d

(B)  **1** -Colonel Adye    **2** -the invisible man
**3** -Colonel Adye    **4** -Dr. Kemp
**5** -the policeman

P. 113   (C)  **1** (c)    **2** (b)    **3** (a)

(D)  **2** → **1** → **4** → **6** → **5** → **3**

P. 128   (A)  **1** turned up high    **2** being violently pushed
**3** What should have    **4** could no longer
**5** whole country knew of
**6** walked over a road that
**7** swung through the air

(B)  **1** The tramp knew it was an invisible man who was talking to him from the beginning. (F)
**2** When Dr. Kemp entered his room, he could see the invisible man lie on his bed. (F)
**3** The invisible man attacked the owner of the costume shop and disguised himself. (T)
**4** Dr. Kemp suggested that dogs be used to try to catch the invisible man. (T)
**5** The invisible man killed the housekeeper who was delivering a note to the Colonel. (F)

P. 129   **C** **1** Why did Mrs. Hall want the stranger to stay at her inn? (c)

**2** What was one of the biggest problems for Griffin when he was outside? (b)

**D** **1** The invisible man took Dr. Cuss's and the reverend's clothes.

**2** The invisible man demanded that the tramp should help him.

**3** A dog came up to the invisible man and bit his leg.

**4** Dr. Kemp met the invisible man in his room.

**5** The invisible man stole money from a bank.

**3** → **1** → **2** → **5** → **4**

隱形人【二版】
**The Invisible Man**

作者 _ 赫伯特・喬治・維爾斯
　　　（Herbert George Wells）
改寫 _ Louise Benette, David Hwang
插圖 _ Julina Alekcangra
翻譯 _ 羅竹君
編輯 _ 賴祖兒 / 羅竹君
作者 / 故事簡介翻譯 _ 王采翎
校對 _ 陳慧莉
封面設計 _ 林書玉
排版 _ 葳豐 / 林書玉
製程管理 _ 洪巧玲
發行人 _ 周均亮
出版者 _ 寂天文化事業股份有限公司
電話 _ +886-2-2365-9739
傳真 _ +886-2-2365-9835
網址 _ www.icosmos.com.tw
讀者服務 _ onlineservice@icosmos.com.tw
出版日期 _ 2021年1月 二版一刷 (250201)
郵撥帳號 _ 1998620-0 寂天文化事業股份有限公司

Adaptors of "*The Invisible Man*"

Louise Benette

Macquarie University (MA - TESOL)
Sookmyung Women's University,
English Instructor

David Hwang

Michigan State University (MA, TESOL)
Ewha Womans University, English Chief
Instructor
CEO at EDITUS

國家圖書館出版品預行編目資料

隱形人/Herbert George Wells原著 ; Louise Benette /
David Hwang改寫. -- 二版. -- [臺北市] : 寂天文化事業
股份有限公司, 2021.01
　　面；　公分
譯自 : The Invisible Man
25K+寂天雲隨身聽APP版

ISBN　978-986-318-960-2 (平裝)

1. 英語　2. 讀本

805.18　　　　　　　109021165